Bite the Big Apple
Baby Girl Book
IV

In the Beginning Book I
Moonlighting in Paris Book II
City by the Bay Book III
Bite the Big Apple Book IV
Caribbean Heat Book V
Return to the Bay Book VI
Prison of the Past Book VII
Baby Girl Box Set - a collection of books I-IV

Elle Klass

Copyright © 2014 by Elle Klass
Published 2020 Books by Elle, Inc.
ISBN: 978-1-951017-16-3
All rights reserved
Editors: Dawn Lewis
Cover art created by Manuela Cardiga
For more information go to
https://elleklass.weebly.com

Books by Elle, Inc.
225 College Dr. #65504
Orange Park, FL 32065
Booksbyelle10@gmail.com

Author's Disclaimer

This book is entirely fictional. Any characters, places or events are purely figments of the author's imagination. No part of this publication may be reproduced, transmitted or redistributed either in its entirety or in part without the author's express written consent.

Other Young Adult Books by Elle Klass

St. Augustine Novellas
Bloodseeker Series
Book 1 The Vampires Next Door
Book 2 The Monster Upstairs
Book 3 The Ghost Within

hidden journals
Isandro
Alarico

Zombie Girl
Book 1 Premonition
Book 2 Infection
Book 3 Retribution

City by the Bay Recap

In City by the Bay, Cleo takes the puzzle pieces involving her mysterious past and begins to link them together. She changes her identity to Shanna Nu and gains employment at the La Tige Detective Agency. She learns Perdy kidnapped her to hide her from the Briggses. A wealthy, powerful family. To give Perdy's family closure, she visits them. Her mother, Leila, is still alive and welcomes Shanna into her home under the pretense that Shanna is a police officer. Shanna shares details of Perdy's death and leaves her with a number to call so she can claim and properly bury her daughter.

Shanna and La Tige become closer than coworkers. She begins to think of him as the father she never had. Likewise, he becomes attached to her. He drops clues involving her past but under no circumstances will she discuss it with him. After solving a big case, he gives her the key to his unsolved cases drawer. She digs through the files finding new information pertaining to Perdy's case along with an unrelated case involving a young woman, a baby, and a police officer. She takes the information and decides to seek employment within the Briggs's infrastructure and go to New York.

Meanwhile, she has become best friends with Kacy, owner of the Happy Trails bar, and her roommate. In Happy Trails late one night she meets Fetch, a gorgeous hunk of man. Her and Fetch form a relationship of sorts. She is unable to trust in their relationship and leaves him, without warning, for New York. She says goodbye to Kacy and La Tige. Before boarding the plane, she finds a note from La Tige in the phone he gave her. It is the address to a rent-controlled apartment.

Miss Executive Secretary

A few drops of wine swirled in the bottom of my glass. I tapped my phone's speaker icon to free my hands and refill the glass. Kacy's voice filled my small rent-controlled studio apartment - a tip from La Tige, my ex-boss and father figure in my life...

"Girlie, how'd you land this fantastic new job?" Kacy and I spoke once a week, sometimes more. I found it refreshing to keep a friend while at the same time disturbing. I never kept relationships of any kind, except James.

"His bulldog of a wife, she looks like a bulldog, jaw jowls, bent arms, the whole works. It met her during the annual Christmas party. She walked inside at the same time I walked outside for fresh air. The night air was warm for December in New York. She slammed into me and I flew backwards into the trash can. Thank God it was lidded or I would've been sitting in it."

"She didn't! I woulda kicked her bulldog..."

"I'm not done. She scowled on the way inside, never turning her head mind you, 'I hope that orange mop isn't natural, you're a disgrace to the company'".

"I totally woulda chased her down and whooped on that rich bully ass." The tension in her voice obvious.

"I'm sure you would have, but I'm classier than that."

"Whatever! Miss-I-left-my-boyfriend without sayin' a word." I heard Kacy chuckling on the other end and detected a slight hesitation in her voice.

"You told him, didn't you?" My voice laced with angst over a man who wasn't my boyfriend. At least we never voiced the words. Fetch was a play guy, simmering hot, but no life goals. I refilled my wine glass again and allowed the sweet red juice to drizzle down my throat.

"I didn't... You got me, I did. But only that you took a better job in New York. I didn't give him your address or anything."

"Some best friend you are!" The two times Fetch called I ignored the rings, allowing the calls to go to voice mail, but he left none.

"He's like the hottest guy ever. He comes into the bar like a broken puppy, droopy eyes, no spark. I'm a sucker for puppies and I told." Kacy was a sucker sometimes, but she hadn't watched a boyfriend, my Einstein, get jolted across the road during a hit and run and die in front of her eyes or stood her next lover, Didier, up on the altar because she pretended to be something she wasn't. No, that was me. A broken home led to my broken life which I desperately tried to fix.

"I'd kick your butt if I was there."

Silence filled the air for thirty seconds before Kacy replied.

"Sorry sweet. I think he's in love with you. The two of you make the best couple I've ever seen."

"I know and I'm not angry. I... He never said the words. If I'm meant to be with Fetch it'll work its way out, somehow, someday. If not, then we aren't meant for each other."

"You are a romantic fool. Sometimes you gotta take life by the horns and just do it." Sentiment crawled into each of Kacy's words.

Desperate to get off the Fetch topic I rerouted the conversation. "After bulldog slammed into me, William III unplastered me from the trash can. We talked. Would you believe his parents refused to let him watch movies like the Wizard of Oz or Oliver Twist when he was a kid?"

"No freakin' way!" The volume of her voice almost burst my ear drums.

"Yes freakin' way, according to him his parents said those movies were too scary and would give him nightmares. Instead, his parents forced him to watch the news or the stock market."

"No Sesame Street?"

"None! I'm surprised he turned out so normal." Not that I watched Sesame Street either but I wished I had.

"My mind is blown. Poor deprived children. How many kids are there again?"

"William III is the oldest Briggs child, then Patrice and last Candace."

"I'm shocked they made it to adulthood." We both chuckled at her response. "Keep going babe, wanna hear the rest."

"I went home and Monday, when I arrived at work, I had an email from him to meet at Vinny's New York Style Brick Oven Pizza House. He sent directions.

"An unhappily married man wanting lunch with a receptionist. All kinds of thoughts and images went through my mind."

"Creeepy."

"Exactly. OK, we met for lunch. I was tense and ready to run thinking affair no way! Turns out he asked me to be his executive secretary. You already know I accepted. The best part, my pay has tripled!"

"Luck finds you. Got no complaints. Love my bar, my bar is my life. No, that's not true - Javier is my life."

"Incorrect, the bar is your life, Javier is secondary." The chilly air brought scents of various cuisines into my apartment through the open sliver of my window. They mingled with the garlic smell from the Italian chicken I cooked for dinner.

"He is not. He's busy with school all the time and the bar... I love the bar, the people... its home." She meant that as she grew up above the bar. During the time we lived together, I saw similarities in our lives, although hers was a lot more normal than mine. I lived in a shack with a junkie fake mom who went missing and turned up dead floating in the Bay just beyond the mouth of

the Sacramento River. That life did a
number on me and pushed me to grow up
long before my time. Kacy grew up above a
bar with a happy family, even so she grew
up quick.

"You're hopeless. Javier will marry you
one day and the two of you will stroll off
into the wild blue yonder together,
forgetting the rest of us."

"So not true. My bar will be the milk
and bread of our marriage if it ever
happens. At least until he gets a job that
pays enough, and we can raise a family. And
you'll be the Maid of Honor at our
wedding."

"Who is the hopeless romantic now?" I
recognized how much she adored every
millimeter of Javier.

"I totally love you Shanna." My body
cringed at that name, not that I hadn't
gotten used to it but I wanted to be me,
Cleo. Not Shanna or Justine or even my
mom's name for me, but Cleo - short for
Cleopatra, as Einstein put it. I needed to
face facts - I would always love the one I
could never have. Slug ruined his life, our
life. My love whom one day I would meet
again if there was a heaven. I desired to tell
Kacy everything. She was my best friend,

only I didn't understand the entire story yet. What would I say? At this point I understood the Briggs' hired Slug as a 'hit man' and my kidnapper-fake-mom-junkie Perdy stole me to protect me from evil powerful people who hunted me.

"Kacy, you are the best friend ever." And one day I will tell you the entire story.

Meet the Briggses

Since coming to New York, I changed my appearance choosing to be careful, more than ever, as my enemies lived close. To disguise my eye color, I wore brown contacts. I paid a visit to a salon, and the beautician colored my hair a less obnoxious shade of orangey-yellow. I added fake nails and wore plenty of makeup. Between the makeup and nails I looked the part.

I got much better insight to the entire Briggs family working for William III - he preferred Will. He was a thirty something good-looking, small built man with light blond thinning on top hair. He stood 5'9, maybe 5'10, slim, with fine features. His hazel eyes like a mood ring changed from brown to green. Green meant happy, carefree, and brown meant stress, trouble.

His wife stopped by the office and called millions of times every day. He asked me to lie and use the 'he's in a meeting or with a client' excuses. She was always rude and muttered ugly comments about me under her breath as she hung up the phone.

He spent his days in his office with the door closed. I wasn't sure what he did but his office stayed quiet and people didn't come and go very often. I figured he earned the position in the family business because he was family. His job consisted of nothing, and he spent his work time sleeping. After all, there wasn't anything for him to do because I did everything.

His wife's build and face reminded me of a bulldog. They were an unlikely couple with no children. I thought children might give her something to do rather than harass him 24/7. She stayed involved in charities and fundraisers, the country club, everything rich people do; somehow though, she didn't stay busy enough. I liked Will, but I didn't like his wife. Hate would be too strong a word to describe my dislike for her but disgust fit.

Six weeks after accepting my new position I experienced the family. Will invited me to their beach mansion in the Hamptons for a family/business weekend. First I met William II, Will's father, he was retirement age, 65 or so. His scalp bald on top, with wisps of dark hair framing his head. Unlike his son he had a large build. Like Will his hazel eyes displayed his moods. He could be gruff but well-mannered in social activities; intelligent, controlling and demanding. Nobody crossed him instead they treated him with respect.

Daddy William II's wife, Carol, was petite and quiet, but professional and all business. Candace, Will's youngest sister, didn't get involved in the family business. She spent her time cavorting with Will's wife, planning and plotting social activities. Candace stood tall like her father but otherwise looked much like her mom. Her husband was a lawyer who worked for Mitchell Strat, the lawyer who always got Slug, Einstein's killer, off the hook. I wondered if she knew what a scum sucking pig her husband worked for?

Patrice took after William II, in a non-married female form, cunning, manipulative and meticulous. No doubt her IQ shot above the 130 plus range. She wanted the business and planned on running it like her dad - without scruples. She wore short, dark hair in a boy cut. Her build petite and her glare equivalent to my body being sawed in two pieces with a dull blade. I saw a resemblance in me to Patrice and William II

- cunning and meticulous, minus the nasty attitude.

I did the job Will paid me for and observed the behavior of his dysfunctional, powerful, rich family. Like a scientist I studied them analyzing the results and concluded I liked Will, but not the rest of the family. He treated others with respect, including his disgruntled bulldog wife.

As much as possible I stole away from the mansion and walked the million-dollar-home beach. Will stayed occupied with his father and Patrice. After dinner the final night while I sat alone on a designer beach recliner listening to the waves William II joined me without an invitation.

"Beautiful isn't it? My children used to run in and out of the tide right here." His eyes gazed upon the vast ocean before us.

"Lucky kids."

"What about you? What's your story?" Wisps of his thin hair blew over the top of his bald head.

I assumed he was prying more than making conversation. I didn't feel up to another story and wished he leave. His presence ruined the serenity the beach offered. "Don't have one. Normal girl, normal life."

"Everyone has a story."

I smiled and sucked in a deep breath of fresh air. "It'd bore you." To heck if I was going to make up another story to feed his meddlesome curiosity.

"You're the first secretary William's had that is capable of the job."

A compliment? "Thank you, Will... William is easy to work for."

He raised his eyebrows and opened his mouth to continue the conversation when my phone rang. I swiped the talk button. "Hey sis, hold on one second."

I slid my phone away from my ear and apologized to Mr. Briggs. "My sister, I gotta go. Thanks for the weekend. Your home is gorgeous."

He munched his eyebrows into a V and punched his lips together as if upset by my actions. I figured not many people walked away from him.

"Kacy, I'm back."

"Did I hear thanks for the weekend? You have a beautiful house. New guy?"

"No! My boss's father. Will brought me to the beach house this weekend for their annual family/business get-together..."
Saved by Kacy.

R. T. P Burke Childrone A. K.A. Einstein

I visited Einstein or rather his burial spot. On Sunday mornings, when everyone else went to church, I spent time with Einstein. Sometimes, I sat beside his grave and cried. I missed the chance to grieve his being taken from me by the ugly monster Slug (Frank Tomey). One Sunday I didn't make it until late in the afternoon and his family was there. Or at least I suspected it was his family. The man and woman looked like older versions of Einstein. I saw them and sat on a bench a few feet away. They brought flowers and laid them on his grave. After a long time, they left. I finished my weekly visit and grabbed a coffee. I came by more often hoping to one day build up the courage to speak. On the day I least expected while visiting during the week, after work, I sat beside his grave deep in thought when a voice startled me out of my Einstein reverie.

"Were you friends with my son?" I looked up from my solace to see his mother. Her hair the same shade of blond as Einstein's only with streaks of white. The skin around her gentle eyes bore webs in the creases. She too was tall and thin. He looked much like her.

"No, we never met, but I heard what happened. I think it... is heartbreaking... what happened. I had a friend who... I just wanted to visit and pay my respects." My brain screamed to tell her 'yes, I loved your son' but I couldn't force my mouth to form the words. Instead, I spun another tale.

"My son was a very special young man. He wanted to do incredible things." *He did something incredible*. Einstein loved and took care of me, but I didn't say that.

"Do you mind me asking...? Why he ran?" The questions streamed out of my mouth like water from a hose. I kicked myself mentally for being so insensitive.

"That is not your business." The pain in her eyes evident, although she didn't ask me to leave. Maybe she needed to talk about it, wanted to talk about it. Every day my heart yearned for Einstein and I needed to talk about it and didn't want her running off so I continued.

"I'm sorry. I had a friend who ran and I don't understand why kids leave a good home. You seem like such a nice woman, a good mother. My friend had a good family but still he ran."

I breathed a silent sigh of relief when she continued. "It seems ridiculous now. I can't forgive myself. We didn't always see eye to eye with Burke." For a long time, we stood there, saying nothing, each of us deep in our own sorrow for the same lost young man.

The silence ended when she spoke. "His dreams that didn't fit our plan, our goals for him. We mapped out his life. He couldn't make a move without us. He dreamed of joining the FBI but we refused to let him follow those dreams. Instead we have a business and planned it on passing to him. I guess we tried to control his life too much." Tears rolled down her cheeks, and I held her in my arms. At that moment I felt closer to her than I ever felt to Perdy. We stood there for what seemed like an eternity but in reality, not more than a couple of minutes. He'd never mentioned he wanted to join the FBI. Einstein and I didn't discuss our past lives only our current and future lives. Our dreams squashed by Slug.

She regained composure and said, "Thank-you. I needed that."

"Would you like to join me for some coffee? Latte Latte is just two blocks south?"

She narrowed her eyes, as if deciphering whether to trust me. "Yes, yes. My treat."

We walked to the coffee shop and talked. I told her about my friend, Einstein, and she told me about Burke. We were two women grieving over the same unforgettable young man - my secret. My time spent with Mrs. Childrone gave me closure. His family wasn't the nightmare family I thought they were. They made a mistake and had to live with it much like my mom, Perdy's, mother Leila.

I needed my encounter with Mrs. Childrone. The mystery of my existence wasn't the only one in my life. I always wondered about his family and pictured them with drawn in frowny lips, hate filled eyes, and nasty demeanors. His mother's sweet personality and motherly face gave me answers to at least one of my life's stories. Mr. and Mrs. Childrone owned a large publishing house. She offered me a card, when we parted and on it, she wrote her personal email.

Daddy Briggs' Secrets Exposed

Will came to work with eyes the color of night – the world's clue of his frustration. He went straight into his office without closing the door as usual and dropped into his chair like a sack of bricks. I walked to his wet bar; poured him an I'm-upset-and-need-a-drink brandy, set it on his desk and turned to leave.

"Don't leave. Close the door and take a seat." My stomach did nervous flip flops as I followed his directions.

He picked up his brandy, swirled it around then looked at me. "I trust you. I can't put my finger on it, but I trust you. Maybe... because you're the only secretary I've had that isn't afraid of my father."

He opened his mouth to continue but stopped short. His eyes penetrating mine. "No, it's more than that. Did you know you twitch your nose the same as Candace when you're deep in thought? Your lips curl like my father's when you smile and well...

you are as fastidious and clever as Patrice and my father. If the three of you got together your power would be unstoppable like the Fantastic Four. You'd be the ahh… Treacherous Three. But you're not like them either. You have heart."

Why was he telling me this? I didn't understand the references to his family and commonalities we shared, although I noticed it myself. I was having a La Tige moment as words stopped short of my mouth leaving me speechless. We sat quiet for a couple of minutes until he spoke again.

"What I'm trying to say is I trust you and I need someone to talk with. I sense I can talk to you and it won't go any further than these four walls." He slammed his empty brandy glass onto his desk.

"I'm flattered." I got up and poured him another brandy and set it on his desk. Then I made myself comfy on his brown leather couch. He stood up, turned his back towards me, walked to his bookshelf, and stared at the books for a minute. He grabbed a leather-bound book, walked towards me and accompanied me on the couch. Clueless as to his point my belly felt like a school of fish with no water were jumping around in it. I dealt with a lot and very few times had ever found myself speechless or nervous. This was one of those rare moments.

His eyes focused on the leather-bound book, he continued. "You've spent enough time with my family to see what they're like. Candace doesn't care. She wouldn't have gone to college if our parents hadn't forced her hand by taking her out of the will until graduation. Patrice wants the business. She is her daddy's child. Like him in every way. I'm the oldest. The largest share of the business is mine." He raised his face. His eyes meeting mine. The darkness in them vanished, replaced with a greenish brown.

"Patrice is fighting to gain control, like my dad, she's heavy handed and takes drastic measures to gain what she desires. My father is a powerful man and uses extreme measures. He is ruthless in business dealings. I've made more money for the company than Patrice because I care. People prefer to deal with me over Patrice and my father. Any business needs a firm hand and a kind voice to survive. I've spent many years and countless hours working to achieve trust and respect, not fear. Fifteen years ago, my father's dirty deals nearly shut the company down. That's when I took over. Patrice threatens to take away what I've worked for and place us back on the "blacklist". On top of that, my wife is convinced I'm having affairs."

Affairs in the plural I voiced in my head. I didn't understand why he married bulldog and why he didn't cheat on her. The fact is he didn't – faithful until the end.

He gulped while his eyes still drove hard into mine. "I've never cheated on my wife. I'm not my father. He always has another woman. He sets them up in penthouses and townhouses across the city and surrounding areas. Yes, my mom is aware. She has always known but remains quiet. Out of fear she won't rock the boat. He takes care of his women until he gets bored and finds another. He doesn't even try to hide his affairs from us. Here, take a look." He handed me the leather-bound book. Inside was a list, printed from the computer, containing women's names and addresses; like he said across the city and surrounding areas. Was he hinting that Daddy Warbucks, I mean daddy Briggs, was my father? He drank his brandy, then got up and slammed the glass hard on his desk.

"I'm not like him!" He didn't have to convince me, I already knew. He was the only humane member of his family. At this point my silence ended. I couldn't stand to see him be so hard on himself and I really, really didn't like his wife. I debated on telling him that but opted to be more professional.

"Your wife is a demanding woman and I imagine high maintenance. Maybe she just needs your affection; a weekend at a bed and breakfast or a cruise, something that puts her first."

He twisted his lips in a sideways smile. "You don't believe that?" No, I didn't. I dealt with the bulldog woman several times daily playing interference for him and wanted her gone. A few unpleasant scenarios involving her drifted through my mind.

"No, I don't. I think you should divorce her. She harasses you daily, and it interferes with my job." Nice Cleo... I needed to get that off my chest and it came as a relief to him as his sullen mood brightened. His eyes green as the rainforest.

He jumped out of his seat. "I'm taking a day off and you're coming with me."

We ended up golfing and having fun. I offered to drive the golf cart - easier to handle then La Tige's beast-vehicle on the hilly streets of San Francisco.

My game was rusty unlike his but we used a similar technique. As two teenagers playing hooky from school, we golfed the day away. I chuckled at how I assumed he wanted an affair with me when he asked me to lunch.

While we played, my mind replayed our discussion. How I reminded him of his family. I considered his dad's list of kept women which I stashed in my purse. He wanted me to have it. Did daddy Briggs' list connect me to him by way of an affair?

"Will, what happened fifteen years ago?"

"Nothing you need to worry over. I soaked a PR and financial fire with water."

Mr. Dancy Eyes

The following day, upon returning from lunch, a man dressed in straight blue slacks with a white buttoned shirt was waiting in the office, reading a paper. As I came through the door, he stood, turned towards me, nodded his head my direction acknowledging my existence then sat in the seat. A shockwave of terror went down my spine and I froze. The creepy man, Mr. Dancy Eyes, who sent Halette's body down the river. He found me!

In New York, I survived in the pit of the lion's den – dodging blows and hiding in corners to avoid being the Briggses next meal. I carried a knife housed in my purse. My mind replayed the self-defense skills Sam taught me in Paris. They hadn't failed me yet, although a six-foot man would be more difficult to take down than a five-foot woman. I wasn't going without a fight. I kept my purse close. Frogs jumped around my belly and my lunch threatened to use my organs as a launching pad. I inhaled deep filling my lungs with the sweet scent of wildflowers from the air fresheners I placed in the office. I hid my nervousness. "Do you have an appointment sir?"

He placed his paper on the chair beside him and stood. I braced myself. "Yes, I'm Mitchel Strat I spoke with William this morning. He asked me to meet him here at one o'clock." His eyes bounced in their sockets making it difficult to discern if he looked at me but the left side of his lips curling upward in a quirky sly smile gave away his recognition.

"He isn't back from lunch yet. Please take a seat." I offered taking my own seat behind my large solid oak desk then dropped my purse into the desk drawer and slipped the knife out. I placed it on top of my purse while leaving the drawer open a sliver. My body cringing in apprehension I crammed my fears into the back of my mind and did my job. "Would you like a water while you wait?"

"No, thank you." He took his seat and went back to reading his paper. I let out a sigh and got to work, keeping a close eye on him. He didn't look my way again. I remembered how he dropped Halette's body in the river to cover my crime, which probably meant he wasn't here to hurt me. None the less, I kept an eyeball glued to him and my blade close.

A few minutes later Will strolled through the door in a much better mood than the previous day, his eyes shining brilliant green. They spoke no words as they strolled into his office and closed the door behind them. Why is this man here to see Will? Is he one of his dad's henchmen? Has Will gone to the dark side? After approximately fifteen minutes the man emerged and strolled out of the office followed by Will. He apologized for not warning me. I guess he recognized my discomfort.

After Mr. Strat left, Will shifted his eyes towards me. His gaze intense. "He's a detective who works for the family. I've hired him to follow my wife, and I don't care if she is having an affair, I want her to wallow in guilt." He whistled "You Are My Sunshine" and strode into his office.

Now I understood, like a lightning bolt hit my brain. I got it! The family hired him to follow me; not kill me. That had been Slug's job, and he failed so he paid the price. The hidden story of my life unraveled in front of me. One piece still didn't make sense - why did he cover my crime?

I checked out daddy Briggs' extensive list of women. At home I researched more information about them, birthdays, where they worked and I found them on social networking sites. My detective skills came in handy. Thank you La Tige!

After work I strolled by their homes, followed them to work when possible. I pulled my own stakeouts compelled by my own curiosity. Their ages spanned a couple decades and each exotic looking. None of them more than my height and weight, five feet, approximately 110 to 120 pounds, dark skin tones with matching dark hair. Minus the orangey hair coloring and brown contacts, I fit the profile. One of these women was my mother and William II was my father.

I looked through their ages and matched them against my birth date. They were either too young or too old with brown eyes. I had green eyes. If William II was my father, I would have a gene for green eyes from him, but my mom would also have green eyes, a brown eyed gene would be dominant. With my sixth-grade education I surmised my mother had green eyes and none of these women did. I was missing one. Maybe on another list that Will didn't know of? One daddy Briggs kept more private.

Call Me Cleo the Stalker

A late April evening I followed the trail of one of Daddy Briggs' women. A beautiful middle-aged brunette with thick hair that hung in loose curls which bounced as she walked and shined from the streetlights. She sauntered into a high-class bar. I followed her inside and took a seat at a booth beside a window.

She strode beside a gentleman with salt and pepper hair and kissed him on the cheek. He took her light jacket and hung it on the back of her chair. She then sat down and he pushed her chair in and ordered two martinis. I attempted the difficult trick of reading her lips but succumbed to reading her body language - much easier.

I calculated a 99% chance she wasn't my mother. Age-wise there was a small possibility, but her brown eyes shrunk that possibility to almost nil. She was a gorgeous fifty-eight who looked thirty-eight. No doubt Botox and/or facelifts played a part.

I grew bored watching them and their love-bird-high-class person etiquette. My eyes wandered outside, cars and taxis zoomed by, people walked past the bar. When the current flood of street people passed the window, I noticed an art gallery across the street. The paintings in the windows caught my eye. One stood out amongst the rest.

"What would you like to order?" Came a sweet voice attached to a young woman no more than twenty-five.

"Nothing thanks." I grabbed my phone and pretended to have a text. "I'm at the wrong place. So sorry." I slipped out of my seat and drifted to the gallery across the street.

The outstanding artwork that captivated my eye was a vivid full color painting of me! I stood gawking at it for several minutes. Memories flooded my mind. I remembered the sketch, flipping through his book. I wandered inside the gallery.

Dumbfounded I stared at each piece of priceless work, my mind reeled with memories. Each piece priced far out of my wallet-zone but their sentiment made them above any price that could be paid.

"Would you like a Kleenex for that drool?" Said the sexy voice of the artist, Fetch.

I spun on my heels to look at him. My eyes big as saucers. "I... How..." I was speechless again!

"I knew I'd find you if I came to New York." He said as if the world revolved around us.

"That... that doesn't even make sense." I stammered.

"Sure it does. My painting. The one of you. The one you were staring at outside the window it caught the eye of a wealthy art dealer. He offered to hang my paintings in his gallery in New York." He said this matter-of-factly as if he always expected to just 'be discovered'.

"There are tons of artists out there. Who?"

"I don't know. I didn't meet the gallery owner. No, I lied. I met his dealer." Dealer, he made it sound like a drug transaction.

"Conveniently you're discovered by someone who owns a gallery in New York?" I gave him the evil eye.

"You should be happy." His silver bullets drilled into my heart and his smell drove me wild. I took a step back, trying to keep myself from doing something I'd regret later.

He took a step forward and then another. Before I knew what was happening, he folded me into his arms and leaned down and kissed my orange less-moppy head. "I missed you. This was a great opportunity and I'm making a lot of money. Be happy for me." He took my head in his hands and kissed my face. His gentle touches lingering on my skin, making their way to my mouth. His tongue found mine. My mind wanted to resist but my body dripping in desire yielded. I wanted him.

A sudden round of applause vibrated my ear drums. We became center stage instead of his paintings. "This delicate flower is my model." He stated then moved aside so everyone could ogle me, giving me Justine, my Paris persona, flashbacks.

He took my hand, and we fled out the door. I was still in a state of shock, or at least I attempted to convince myself of that. The truth was I missed him and being so close, feeling his tender embrace and smelling his Fetch-ness was too enticing. I lost my will power.

We ended up in his hotel room. His spell wiped my mind - powerless to resist.

In the elevator, down the halls, he continued kissing me, gentle touches played across my skin and lips. We burst into his room, leaving a trail of clothes behind us. We didn't even make it to the bed. Instead, he hoisted me onto the dresser, where I reached the point of ecstasy at least once. Then he lifted me up tossing me onto a soft, padded, roomy chair where he continued his delightful assault on my body.

Wore out, we made it to the bed where we lay quietly, catching our breath.

"Your picture, I hung it at Happy Trails. A man came in and took pictures of it. I asked him what he thought he was doing. He said, 'Do you know the artist?' I said, 'Yeah, you're looking at him.' He asked me if I'd take half a million for the painting. I told him it wasn't for sale and he left." I listened as he continued the story.

"He comes in again the next night and offers me double. I tell him the same thing. He hands me a card and leaves. Two days later he shows up again and says, 'I sent the pictures of this painting to my benefactor who is willing to pay you five million for that painting'. I told him, 'It's not for sale!' By this time, I was angry, so he says, 'Six million and we'll hang it along with your

other paintings in his gallery in New York.'"
He stopped there and thrust his tongue
inside my mouth.

"Stop, my will power is back." I jostled
him away from me.

"OK, I ask him what's in it for me
besides the six million. He offers to pay me
huge royalties on everything I sell. I figured
why not? Maybe if I'm rich you'll want me
again." I didn't like his insinuation I only
dated rich guys? I grew up eating out of
dumpsters, living on the streets and
dropped my multi-billionaire fiancé to seek
the answers to my own existence that have
intrigued and scared me throughout life!
My anger subsided and a part of me wanted
to forget everything and stay with him
forever.

I grabbed the pillow under my head
and hit him with it. He returned fire. "You
are full of shit." I choked out between
laughs during our pillow fight.

"Am not, this benefactor guy
transferred me six mill for that painting and
high royalties on everything sold. I never
have to work a real job again. I can spend
my time with you and paint." He was
delusional, absolutely delusional.

"Who is the benefactor?"

"I don't know but he pays me well so I don't care. I'll take my money and travel the world." He said as if he had it all planned.

"It seems too weird. A guy sees the painting in a bar and wants it. He pays you more money than any average American makes in a lifetime for a single painting and you don't question it. Whose name is on the card? What did he look like?"

"He was a big guy, looked like a linebacker. Had a square shaped jaw, and the weird thing, his lips barely moved when he spoke. He looked like a ventriloquist's dummy." Fetch imitated the man, "Like this," barely moving his jaw as the words found their way out.

I laughed picturing Sam. He did a great impression. Didier was an art freak. He loved paintings and Fetch just described Sam. I wasn't sure why he'd be looking for me now or perhaps he was just keeping tabs on me like he always did. If Didier wanted to find me no hiding space on Earth existed that I could hide from Sam.

He pulled me on top of him and mumbled between kisses and heated breaths, "Now I can have you."

I ignored his words as my body relented to his touch.

Four thirty in the morning while Fetch slept soundly, I slipped off the bed and stumbled into my clothes. I kept one eye on him, his long, brown tufts draped over his face, the sheet covered his torso while his toned legs peeked out from underneath and his feet hung over the edge of the bed. Every part of my body screamed at me *stay* but my brain said *go*. I tiptoed to the door and left.

Calling in a Favor

My night with Fetch left me frazzled. My thoughts drifted to our shameless night of ecstasy. His scent and silver bullets lingered in my mind. I wanted him in the worst way possible. Will discerned my apparent uneasiness and offered, "You need a day off? So do I. Let's golf."

This go around I was on my game. Like two kids in heavy competition we resorted to cheat-like tactics running amok on the golf course. A beer for each hole in one. We grew tipsy, or at least I did, by the time we finished. Somehow the more beer I drank, the better my golfing game. We stopped at Sushi House for dinner then he took me home. The bond between Will and I continued to grow, each day I saw him in a new light. My original perception he slept all day instead of work changed. He liked fun but also lived and breathed business. Play time equaled think time for Will.

It was eleven before I made it to bed.
As I turned in, I checked my phone. One
message from Fetch blinked for my
attention - *???*. I turned off my phone,
flipped on the TV and watched my favorite
show, Frat Squad. It was a reality show
about college students, not just Frat
students. What intrigued me is they were
my age and even though my life went in a
completely different direction I had a lot in
common with them. Tonight though, my
body and mind were so tired I dozed off
into a welcomed sleep.

Over the next few weeks Fetch didn't
text or call back, which made it much easier
for me to concentrate on my search for my
biological mom or bio-mom as I renamed
her. At work I spent as much time as
possible searching the computer. I scanned
through tenants, employees, clients, and
business partner files. The search relentless
buried in the never-ending frustrating list of
names. I wanted the answers, and they
were not forthcoming. To absorb and regain
focus I stepped away and called in a favor.

I sent La Tige the list of women and
asked him to find out what he could and get
back with me. Then I separated myself from
seeking my identity until I heard from him.

The separation lasted a few weeks, not yet ready to return to the overwhelming task. In that time, I worked and came home, cooked, watched TV, and talked with Kacy several times a week. I told her about my romp with Fetch and she informed me he hadn't returned to the bar. A part of me wanted him to be there, another part of me didn't. The night we met played over and over in my head. I desired him sexually more than any man I'd met, even my beloved Einstein.

Past lovers drifted in and out of my thoughts. The fresh scent of Didier's cologne and softness in his accented voice lingered in my memories alongside Einstein and Fetch. The benefactor who paid Fetch the handsome portion of money for his paintings teetered on the edge of my mind and screamed Didier's name. Why after all this time would he try to worm back into my life? I didn't understand and why Fetch? I pressed the start button on my computer and searched for the results of my wedding that never happened. Handsome, wealthy men don't often get left at the altar I'm sure it made the news. I laid the computer on my bed. I knew the results. My computer became a ping pong ball as I picked it up again and found the hotel. Tears gushed from my eyes as I looked through the pictures of rooms remembering my time in Paris as if it happened yesterday. We could have enjoyed a wonderful life together under different circumstances. The phone La Tige gave me rang shocking me out of my delicious and exasperating thoughts.

"What's up?"

"Nu, I'll be your way on Friday. Would you like to meet for dinner?"

"Yeah, where?"

"I'll meet you after work. You choose. See you then." Click. The phone went dead. Typical La Tige. I hoped he had information for me from the list I sent him.

The Missing Piece

True to his word, La Tige waited for me outside my office building Friday evening. We enjoyed a pleasant dinner, and he filled me in on his current cases. He knew the strange ones intrigued me and explained a cheating spouse case he recently closed. Ends up the spouse wasn't cheating but had split personalities. I told him about my job and 'the family'. I gave him a short description of each member. He laughed. I told him how Will and I skipped work and played golf.

After dinner we walked for a while, talking. This was the longest conversation I held with La Tige. Only in town for the day he cut our visit short as he hailed a cab outside my apartment building. He sunk his bulk into the backseat and handed me a folded note. "If you ever need anything, call." He closed the door leaving me steeped in anxiety and the cab took off blending into New York traffic.

I unfolded the note and read the name, Claudel Winters along with her address and phone number. In more La Tige chicken scratch the words *she is expecting you* jumped out from beneath her information. I recognized the name Claudel Winters - she was an employee of the Briggs', now retired. I saw her name while snooping through the computer files.

La Tige would never put me in a place of harm and probably already spoke to her. My guts twisted and wrenched with apprehension. With each step the door to my apartment seemed to grow further away with a final lurch I fell into it taking a deep breath. My hands fumbled inside my purse for the keys until grabbing the familiar clump of metal. Once inside I fell onto the sofa and picked up my phone. My fingers pressed each button in slow motion then a single ring sounded on the other line before I chickened out and pressed the red hang up button. Several minutes passed before realizing my fingers nervous tapping on the coffee table. I looked at my phone and it stared back at me, beckoning me. I clicked Kacy's pic, my finger lingered over the number. One click, but what would I say? I flipped my phone over as questions raced through my head. Is this my bio-mom? Does she know my bio-mom?

In the past, I went for my goals, making up stories to gain information but in this case, I had to be me, Cleo. She may identify me by something else. I took in a deep breath and blew it out. I dreamt of being this close. Now my nerves made the phone call impossible. I grabbed my coat and purse, took one last look at my phone laying silent on the coffee table and jetted out the door as if being chased by a madman.

I needed to take the edge off and walked several blocks. My eyes blind to the change of scenery until the familiarity of fluorescent lights flashed beside me, a bar, that's what I needed. The place wasn't any bigger than Happy Trails and I thought of Kacy. The night I walked into Happy Trails for the first time had been a depressing day. I was apartment hunting with no luck. Kacy's prescription changed everything. Her friendship and a Kacy Cocktail. I pulled up a stool and a young man behind the bar with warm blue eyes and dark hair sticking out in wild curls said, "What'll you have?"

"I need a special order." I rattled off the ingredients, within minutes he worked his magic and served me a chilled Kacy Cocktail.

As I hammered it down, he asked, "So what do you call it?"

I slammed my glass on the counter and asked for another.

"Kacy, is that you?" His warm blue eyes smiled as I responded.

"No, Kacy is my best friend who I truly miss right now. She's a bartender." Best friend, that felt so good to say and I said it without lying. This realization compelled my vocal cords to continue.

"I met Kacy on a bad night. Not unlike tonight. I have an important decision to make."

"That sounds serious. Try me. We bartenders have a secret code that makes us good listeners." His lips curled in a sideways smile and a small dimple showed on his left cheek. He handed me a beer and popped one open for himself. Then he yelled, "Taking a break Cat!" He came around the bar, cupped my hand in his and showed me to a table.

"For the next fifteen minutes, I'm Kacy."

Put on spot by a stranger I stammered, attempting to find the words lodged in my throat. I never told Kacy about the search for my bio-mom. How could I tell a complete stranger and not Kacy? Shouldn't she be the first to know?

He put his hand in front of his face, straightened out his fingers and air filed his nails blowing on them when finished. "Spill girl."

A chuckle rose inside my belly and resounded through my body, coming out in a big belly laugh. Somehow, he kept a straight face and continued to air file his nails.

When I got control of myself, I began my story, well not all of it. "I'm in New York looking for someone. I received a tip and a phone number from a very reputable source but I can't get over my nerves to call the number. For many years I've waited to get this far and now I've lost my nerve. I'm the girl of steel, like superman-ette. My nerves never get the better of me."

"There's always a first, hon. You are two cocktails in, soon three and a beer." He got up and went to the bar returning with two Kacy cocktails and another beer. He handed the drink to me. "Bottoms up!" We took the shots together and chased them with our beer. "Now you have liquid nerves of steel. Pick up your phone and make that call."

I remembered purposely leaving my phone on the coffee table at home. "I can't."

"Liquid nerves of steel babe, sure you can. I'll dial it for you."

"I can't my phone's at home."

"No problem." He whipped his phone out of his pocket with one fluid motion. "What's the number?"

He wasn't Kacy, but a close second, and every bit as demanding. He wouldn't take no for an answer, right now that's what I needed and the liquid nerves of steel helped. I fumbled in my purse and pulled out the number, rattling it off while he dialed. He handed me the phone and walked back to the bar.

The phone rang in my ear. On the fifth ring a woman's soft, sweet voice came over the other end. "Hello."

I took a deep breath and almost hung up, then mustered the courage to say, as she said hello again, "Is this Claudel?"

"It is. Who is calling?"

Her voice was so sweet it beckoned me to continue. "This is Shanna. A Mr. La Tige gave me your number. He said you were expecting my call." I did it and with honesty! The alcohol started too settled in and I struggled to speak coherent words. Warm blue eyes gave me a thumbs up as he eyed me from across the room.

"Oh yes." The smile in her voice shone through her words. "Yes, dear. I have been waiting years for this phone call. It is so wonderful to hear your voice. Can you come over tomorrow afternoon?"

Her grandmotherly voice drew me in stopping me from dropping the phone and running at the 'I have been waiting years' bit.

"How about tomorrow evening after work?"

"That would be wonderful. Did Mr. La Tige also give you my address?"

"He did. About six tomorrow." My liquid nerves of steel changed to inebriated and the room whirled as I clicked the phone off, dropping it on the table.

Warm blue eyes leaped across the bar like a male gymnast exposing his well-defined arms and chest as he rushed to my side.

"What your is name?" I stammered in my inebriated state.

"Glynn."

"I'm Cle-Shan...na"

He put his hand out. "Pleasure to meet you Cle-Shan...na". His warm eyes smiling at me again.

"No, just Shannana. I mean Shan...n...a."

"Shanna, let me call you a cab."

I got up, lost balance and fell back into my seat. "I can walk."

"No, you can't. Do you live far?"

"A slew blocks eats." I managed. Luckily as a bartender he knew a second language - drunk.

"Cat, running out to take a customer home!"

Not in the Cards

Claudel lived in a nice apartment in an older, well-kept building. She probably lived there for years; rent controlled and paid little to nothing every month. I rang the buzzer to her apartment. She answered, I gave her my name, and she rang me into the building. I chose the stairs instead of the elevator to work off me nervous energy.

Small fake plants in the corners, freshly painted walls, and tasteful art completed the décor in her building. It reminded me more of a hotel than an apartment building. I knocked on her door once and she answered right away.

Her gray hair lay in a loose bun with a few stray hairs caressing her neck. She stood several inches taller than me but most people did, her back straight as a flagpole, and she had a certain class about her. "Shanna, it's such a pleasure to meet you." She said, sliding the door further open and used a sweeping motion with her hand to entice me inside her home.

At the moment I felt a little like Gretel from the fairy tale. I followed a trail of breadcrumbs for years and now here I was standing in front of my unknown past or the wicked witch. In the tale of Hansel and Gretel the witch fooled them with candy. Was I being fooled with a sweet old lady act and the promise of answers?

She closed the door behind me and took me in with her eyes. "You have grown to be such a beautiful young woman." Her eyes became deep wells filled with tears. She took both my hands, then wrapped her arms around me. This woman meant nothing to my life, yet I meant something to hers. I met her hug and allowed her to cry. She straightened herself, wiped her eyes and said through broken sobbing, "I'm sorry, please follow me and we'll sit and have a chat. I'm sure you have questions for me."

If I didn't know better, I'd have thought she was my mother, but her skin was too light and her eyes sea blue not green, not to mention she was far too tall. Maybe she was a grandmother?

"Ms. Winters."

She composed herself. "Please excuse my behavior. You must think me a crazy old woman." Her sea blue eyes sparkled under the light.

We sat in the 'parlor', she in a large overstuffed chair with gold trim and me on an overstuffed matching loveseat with gold trim, an oval walnut table sat between us. Tucked into the corner of the room in front of a large bay window sat a large potted plant with peacock feathers. The window covered in cream sheers with many tiny trinkets displayed on the window's shelf finished the motif of the room.

As she poured the tea into delicate cream mugs decorated with pink and purple flowers, I began where I left off, "Ms. Winters, I am confused. I'm not sure what our connection is or how it is you know me?"

"I'm sorry honey. You would be. Please let me start from the beginning, don't hesitate to ask questions. Your mother, Celia, she is a beautiful woman, even now. She has long thick flowing hair of the deepest velvet brown, her eyes the color of emeralds. She is tiny, about your size and build. You look much like her except you bleached your hair and your eyes, they're brown, and" she shook her head slightly, "but your facial features are almost identical." Her face lit up with the mention of my bio-mom. I sat quiet choosing to hear her out as I hoped there was a logical reason she didn't raise me.

"My eyes are green." I took the contacts out.

"Yes, you do - the color of hers. Your father fell in love with her. He truly loved her and couldn't bring harm to her. Mr. Briggs is a frightening man but much a sheep when it came to your mom. His selfish ways stopped him from risking the exposure of an illegitimate child but his love for her obstructed him from harming her." Sure, but he plotted to kill me, their 'love child'? I didn't smile and kept my thoughts to myself.

"How did you meet my parents?"

"I worked for your father, Mr. Briggs." Well, one question answered. Yup, he was definitely my sperm donor, but not my father. "He hired me to cater to your mother's needs. I did it till three years ago when I retired. He gave her the brownstone, just signed the title over to her and kept me there to care for her. We became good friends. I loved my job but your mom was heartbroken when you... disappeared. She kept you against his wishes. She wanted me to be your full-time nanny. He wanted you…" She stumbled on her words for a fraction of a second. Then she brought the delicate teacup to her mouth and sipped.

"He wanted her to get an abortion, but by the time she told him it was too late, her pregnancy in the second trimester. She refused to tell him afraid of his reaction. He was furious. His father was an honest businessman and didn't approve of your father's style of doing business or his philandering. He told him if he fathered an illegitimate child he would lose everything. His wife knew about you, and his affairs but she had dignity and respect. She was, and still is, a pillar of the community, and wasn't about to give that up so she helped with the deception. Your mother and I finished a nursery for you, complete with pink walls, a white crib with matching dresser and a rocking chair. Baby clothes, gowns and designer outfits, filled the dresser drawers. We set up a bassinet next to her bed for you to sleep in at night. She gave you a name, Camille. She loved you and the name. When she felt you move and kick, she got so excited."

"If she loved me so much, why did she let me go?"

Her sea blue eyes grew sad and gray. "It wasn't her choice. She went into labor and I drove her to the hospital. Her labor was long and difficult - 23 hours. You screamed as the doctor placed you on the scale - 5 pounds, 6 ounces, and 18 inches long. The nurse placed you on her chest, for a brief moment, she held you. Her labor took its toll on her body and she needed rest. The nurse wheeled you to the nursery, and I stayed by your mother's side. I've always regretted that I didn't follow you to the nursery, but we never expected what happened to happen. We thought Mr. Briggs came to terms with you. We were dreadfully wrong. Someone stole you from the nursery. Nobody saw anyone come in or leave, you just disappeared. The hospital closed in search of you and the incident made the news but the police and detectives your mother hired didn't find you. Your mother cried for months, she's never been the same. Sometimes she went into the nursery and rocked, staring blankly."

The weight of the world crashed onto my shoulders - hard. My breathing became shallow, and the world turned black before my eyes. I dropped my head between my knees to avoid fainting. "How come, if my mom loved me so much, she never came looking for me?"

"Shanna?" She placed her hand on my back and gently rubbed.

Through my knees, I asked again with more force in my voice. "How come she never came looking for me?!"

She continued her story, my head still between my knees. "Celia went to visit Mr. Briggs. She barged into his office and screamed, 'where is my baby?!' He told her you were dead. She pushed everything off his desk, threw items across his office and hit him with all the power in her tiny fists. He called security, and they pulled her off him and escorted her out of the building. After that, he wired $100,000,000 into her bank account and signed the brownstone over to her. He continued to pay my salary. They never saw each other again. She believed you were dead."

For a brief second I wondered if my present behavior was anything like my bio-mom. Claudel was so fluid with her story. I pressed my head deeper between my legs. The blackness disappeared. I couldn't face the truth. I pictured her a monster who gave me away. My mind refused to accept anything different.

I shot up straight as a La Tige bullet into the heart. "But you knew I was alive, earlier you stated that you expected my phone call for years."

She smiled warmly. "Yes, you're right. Several years ago, I bought a magazine with your picture on it. I showed this to Celia. Her face brightened. I hadn't seen her that happy since your birth. She hired a detective to track you. He found you in Paris, took many pictures of you. He kept a close eye on you and informed us of your pending wedding. Your mother wanted to see you but didn't know how to approach you. She went to Paris and planned on blending in at your wedding but you never showed. You disappeared once again. Her heart broke. She couldn't take the emotional strain anymore. When she returned home, she placed you in the back of her mind.

"What made you think the girl on the magazine was me?"

"When you meet Celia, you will know the answer."

She handed me a card with my mom's name, number, and address. "Your mother would love to meet you. I won't tell her you were here. I understand you must be going through an emotional upheaval right now. Think about it and if you approach her, please be careful. Emotionally, she is fragile." *Her, what about me?*

I felt no remorse for my bio-mother. No one twisted her arm to enter a relationship with a married man and then get pregnant. She understood there would be consequences and paid the price, but so did I more than her. I lived in a shack with a junkie who cared more for my well-being than my own mother who carried me for nine months and gave birth to me. Out of my own curiosity, I wanted to see her, but I didn't want to meet her.

For the next few weeks I went by her townhouse. A bench across the street made a great place to sit and read a magazine without drawing attention. After a few visits I caught sight of her leaving. She got into a waiting taxi. I snapped a picture later comparing it to myself. Unmistakably, I am her child; my hair, build, height - the way she carries her purse. Claudel's description of 'beautiful' didn't describe her stunning appearance. Do people perceive me as gorgeous as her? Thank my goodies I took after her instead of my sperm donor. I didn't understand why a woman who looked like her would bother with a man who looked like Mr. Briggs. I assumed money was the driving factor.

Reality check, I looked too much like her for William II not to discern. I'm sure like Will he picked up on the similarities in expressions and mannerisms. He knew but didn't harm me? Maybe, somewhere underneath his suit of armor protecting him, he developed a heart. It would have been easy to kill a baby he'd never seen but not a full-grown woman who looked like the love of his life. My heart held more anger towards her than him. In their immoral affair I received the short end of the stick.

Sowing What You Reap

I gave Will my two weeks' notice. It was time for me to move on and start the next chapter in my life. It saddened him but he understood and didn't hold me back. However, I had one more huge 'family' charity event to attend on the coming Saturday.

It was more of a high society ball where rich people doled out huge chunks of money to build their egos and appear concerned. I'd joined in similar such events in Paris and hated them. Rich people pretending to do the world a favor because they gave up a few thousand for the common good. None of these people understood how poverty stricken felt, fighting for each meal, and planning how to survive from one day to the next. I believed I left Didier because I didn't know my identity and couldn't continue the rest of my life living a fake life. The truth, I was the farthest thing from a high-life socialite.

The event took place at a huge convention center in Manhattan. As executive secretary I rode in the limo with Will. His bulldog wife went to the event early, so I didn't have to put up with her. The limo pulled up to a huge building made of glass. They rolled the red carpet out as we stepped from of the limo. Paparazzi went crazy with their cameras.

"Shield your eyes." William leaned over and whispered in my ear.

"No kidding. The glass from the building makes the flashes blinding." I whispered back wearing my painted smile.

The event hosts kept the media outside, thank goodness, so once we made it inside the only sharks to fear was the family. My family.

My official job for the company was to be present. The night was mine. I planned on swimming in the opposite direction of the sharks who no doubt wanted to be the center of attention.

The huge potted plants in the corners looked to be a great place to hide. I grabbed a glass of wine and a bite of finger food as I made my way towards them. Once behind a huge ficus tree I spied my surroundings. I felt like a scared little twelve-year-old girl all over again; hiding out in fear of people turning me over to the authorities.

"Why does a woman of your beauty hide behind a tree?"

I didn't hear the footsteps approaching and jumped out of my skin at the sound of the man's voice. I closed my eyes and took in a deep breath. Mr. Dancy Eyes - my nickname for him, Mitchell Strat, stood behind me with a fresh glass of wine in his hand. My heart sunk to my chest, I brought a small handbag with me and my knife was safely at home where I wasn't!

"I didn't mean to frighten you. I saw you standing here alone behind this gorgeous ficus and thought 'that woman needs a drink'."

"Thanks, mine's running empty." I sucked the last drop of sweet red wine. Even though I hypothesized he meant me no harm, my heart dropped to my feet and panic sank into my guts. I did my best to stay calm and casually took the new wine glass he offered and set the empty glass on a server's tray as one flashed by us.

"Are you going to tell me why you're hiding out? Or do I have to torture it out of you?" *Did he just say that?* "I can be very convincing with two feet and a dance." His jovial tone suggested a joke. I didn't find it funny.

"Uh… I'm not hiding, looking for a quiet spot to check my voice mail." I fumbled as my brain searched for a feasible excuse without allowing him to smell my fear.

"I might assume that if your phone rested in your hand but I don't see it anywhere. Join me in a dance and we'll keep your hiding behind the plant our secret?" Classical music played in the background as a variety of bits and pieces of conversations bombarded my ears. He held out his hand in a gesture to lead me to the dance floor.

Without much choice, other than to make a scene, I followed him, placing my undrunk wine on a table. I didn't plan on drinking it anyways, it could have poison or a date rape drug in it. Pictures of him dumping Halette's body in the river raced through my mind. I tried to shake the images from my head, after all he didn't killed her, I did. An unfortunate accident, I lived with every day.

I took a deep breath and decided to 'woman-up'. "Mr. Strat, what is it you want to say?"

He took my right hand and placed his other hand on my back as we danced. "Just a dance."

"Somehow I don't believe that and I'm not sure whether you mean me harm or protection." Truth! I faced my fears and got it out.

He sized me up with his black eyes, one bounced slightly within its socket. "Yes, we have history and far more than you know." What did that mean?

"It was your fight to survive, your will and cunningness that won me." He said, smooth as melted butter on a bagel.

"I'm sooo glad."

"You are owed the truth and I may be the only one to tell you the story." He twirled me under his arm before he led me into a private area. The music a quiet melody.

My heart thumped outside my chest and my brain replayed the self-defense skills Sam taught me.

"Mr. Briggs didn't want you discovered. The plan was for Mr. Tomey to take and dispose of you, but that bit of information isn't news to you?" He voiced in a questioning tone without asking an actual question. "When Tomey came back with your hospital cap Mr. Briggs knew you were still alive and sent me to find you. It took me time to track you down and when I did, you lived a secluded life in Brennan, California, with that unfortunate drug addicted woman. I kept tabs on you until you slipped my grasp and left." My blood boiled as he talked about me and Perdy as if we were both unfortunate wastes of oxygen breathing carbon-based life forms.

"How kind of you!"

"No harm done. Your life was quiet and private. When you slipped my grasp, I had a chase on my hands. My respect for you began that day."

"And Slug?"

His thin lips twisted into a wry smile. "Slug. Mr. Tomey is quite the Slug isn't he. An appropriate nickname. I digress. I knew he'd hang himself. It took a few years to catch up to you, always one step behind, but once you settled with that boy I found you. I admired a child who outsmarted my well-developed detective skills." His arrogance shone through the deep black holes on either side of his large nose. Deep valleys creased his cheeks from a losing battle with acne as a teen. He was uglier up close.

"Are you done?" I blurted out, short and to the point. He caught my arm in his bulky hand as I turned to leave.

"I'm sorry I wasn't able to stop Slug from hitting your boyfriend. That's why I followed you to Paris. As a quiet observer, you won my heart. I couldn't bear for you to be put in harm's way." He stopped, his eyes soft and pleading as though he had more to say. My heart fluttered and tears threatened my eyes as I realized he'd not meant me harm but was the single most reason I was still alive.

He opened his mouth and closed it again, then reopened it. "I convinced Tomey to plead guilty. I can be very," he paused for a second, "convincing." He let go of my arm. I wasn't sure if I should thank him or not.

"Did my bio-mom hire you?"

His thin bird-like lips stretched across his face in a kinda smile. "You've seen your mother?"

"Seen, yes. Met, no." The air between us so heavy I could have chopped it in pieces with an ax.

"Mr. Strat you avoided my question."

"And so I did. Yes, she hired me twice."

"You played both sides. I hope they paid you well." I turned to leave, then paused as I realized I had one more question to ask. "When did my bio-granddaddy die?"

His thin smile a lingering grimace upon his hill and valley face. "Five years ago."

"He never knew I existed?"

He shook his head back and forth. "You are the best kept secret in the family." With bio-granddaddy dead Slug's attempted murder on my life was pointless and personal.

I left the area seeking fresh air to soak in everything he told me. Five years ago I lived a quiet life with Einstein.

After a few steps daddy shark walked towards me. I grabbed a glass of red wine off a server tray. A necessary requirement to listen to the diarrhea that ran from daddy dearest mouth.

"Miss. Nu, have you seen my son?"

At that moment I decided his shirt a better place for my wine and deliberately poured it on his white dress shirt. "You are a bastard and I have no idea how your sperm borne anything worthwhile. It's an enigma how William and I turned out OK." I sauntered off, steam billowing from my ears and radiating off every inch of my body. I didn't look back. I kept walking and hijacked the limo and driver.

Wow! That Felt Good.

I asked the driver to drop me at Glynn's. He was the closest thing to Kacy I had to talk to in person and I craved a face to face.

He saw me coming and threw together a Kacy cocktail as I entered and handed it to me, his wild curls stuck out everywhere. A smile creased his lips. "Salute!"

We downed our shots quick. Soft music played quietly in the background and a few customers littered barstools. Glynn handed me a beer. "What do I owe this pleasure?"

"Everything! A volcano erupted inside me today."

He chuckled. "Would this have anything to do with your phone call the other night?"

"Indirectly."

"I'm all ears." His ears danced as he wiggled them.

I play punched his arm, and we talked on and off for hours. He gave me a ride home again, wanting nothing more than my friendship. We swapped numbers. In my apartment I flopped onto the couch. I learned I had an uglier than sin guardian angel and told off my sperm donor. I had a rough start in life, then lived as a fairy tale princess. Now I was an average woman, more than that, I accomplished a lot with only a 6th grade education. I thought of the students on Frat Squad and wondered if my life experiences counted for a college degree? My eyelids drooped, and I fell asleep on the couch with the TV flickering.

Now that the secret was out, and I took care of William II, two more items on the short list in my head called for my attention so I could be free of my identity crisis. One person I needed to meet; someone who attempted to kill me, who'd never hurt me or anyone else again. The other a personal release.

I faxed La Tige all the information I collected connecting Mr. Tomey to my mother's, Perdy's, murder. I wanted him behind bars for the rest of his life.

For Will, I purchased a miniature motorized golf cart, wrapped it and placed it in my bottom desk drawer with a note that read:

You have been a wonderful employer, a good friend and more than that, a brother. Love Shanna.

Sprinkling Salt on a Slug

My last day, I left the gift in my drawer. Before I left, I gave Will, my brother, a hug. I pulled out my gift for him from the drawer. "For you."

With surprise in his brilliant green eyes, he opened the small gift and read the note. He pulled the golf cart out of the box. "You know, this isn't it. We'll golf again." Then he drew me towards him in a warm brotherly hug.

He brought his arms to his sides then brought one hand to his back pocket and lifted a sealed envelope out of it. "A little something for you, but don't open it until you leave my office."

I brought my eyebrows into a squint, confused why I couldn't open it now. "You'll see why."

I gave him one last quick hug and left. We hadn't said goodbye. That was too final and we would see each other again. Carefully, I shoved the point of my house key under the seal of the envelope and lifted the flap. Inside the envelope was a receipt for a wire transfer to my bank account for the sum of $250,000,000, stock shares in the business and a letter. I dropped to the ground two blocks from work, flabbergasted. $250,000,000 was an incredible amount of money. People walked by me as I sat Indian-style on the sidewalk. "All of Me" by John Legend sounded from my purse and stopped before I realized Fetch was calling me - the last person I wanted to talk to at the moment. I opened the letter. It read...

Shanna,

My little sister, I felt you should receive compensation as a family member. I have given you a few shares. They are the difference in ownership of the company between me and Patrice. Neither of us owns more shares than the other. My father will not object and if he does, it doesn't matter. I have willed to you my entire ownership and shares within the business. If I die you own the controlling factor of shares. My father controlled everything and everyone around him, the more controlling he became, the more everything fell apart. Please accept

the money and the shares from brother to sister. You are my only sister whose presence I enjoy. Until we golf again.
Love William.

I accepted his offer and knew I always had an ally within the structure of 'the family' and William II would say nothing. His son outwitted him. If William II did anything now, his secret would be an open book to the entire world.

I went home and finished packing my bag. I stuffed my laptop into my old backpack and enough clothes in a suitcase to last me a couple weeks.

The next day I boarded a plane to visit the most despicable creature and my nemesis.

Slug

The state penitentiary housing Slug was a solemn building. It stood as an eyesore in the middle of nowhere. A gray stone structure surrounded by electric steel gates wrapped the building like a cage. Inside a gloomy slate blue paint covered the walls, various chips in the paint exposed previous colors. Guards searched me, took and logged in my personal items. A guard walked me to a room and asked me to sit. A layer of thick bulletproof glass separated visitors from the prisoners. From the other side of the glass a guard brought in a prisoner dressed in Jailhouse orange - Slug. He looked like the frightening man in my dreams. His dull brown hair long and stringy and coal black eyes - the gates of hell. He shuffled to a seat across the thick glass from me and picked up a device that looked like the mouthpiece of a phone. I picked up the one on my end.

With a sneer as heavy as a two-ton brick he mimicked, "Well, if it isn't the illegitimate brat in person, you had to experience my magnetic personality face to face?" He seethed between his teeth.

I ignored his comments and got to business. "I'm here to offer you a deal. You are up for parole soon and stand a good chance of getting released. You killed my mom, Perdy. But like me, you are a pawn in my sperm donor's twisted web of lies. I have evidence to prove it and connections with the police. If you answer my questions I won't go to the police with my information, but if you lie or refuse to cooperate, I will see you never get out of this prison." I lied, I already faxed everything to La Tige and upon my word he'd send it to Officer Han. Slug sat in quiet contemplation for a few seconds.

"What do you want?" The right side of his mouth twitched when he spoke.

"I want to hear your side of the story from the beginning when you first met my mom, Perdy."

"That's it?"

"That's it."

With a large sigh and a twitch at the left corner of his mouth, he began his story. "I met Perdy when she was in high school. I dropped out. She was my girl. Her daddy didn't like me though. I wanted to go to New York, she begged to come with me. Her dad was real hard on her, used to beat her up real bad. We left for New York and I met some people, who knew some people who hooked me up with your father." I cringed at the word father. He may have donated sperm but was no father to me. Not even close.

"I never met him face to face, but he paid me well to keep people and things quiet. I did what he asked and kept my mouth closed. The money was good, and I got the protection of 'the family'. Perdy and I lived good, steak every night, she'd get her nails done once a week, and plenty of coke to keep her happy."

I never doubted he was the reason she became a junkie, but hearing it come straight from his vile mouth made me want to twist his tongue in knots and pour sulfuric acid on it. I kept my poker face as I dreamed of his tongue burning from the heavy acid. Slug stretched his back and unused arm then burrowed his coal black eyes straight into my heart.

"Your daddy liked pumping your mom, she ended up pregnant. He didn't want you around and paid me to kill you. I woulda stood out tryin' to take you from the hospital but I knew Perdy could do it without being caught. So, I paid her half the money to snatch you. Problem was, once she snatched you, she refused to give you up and disappeared with you and her half of the money. That wasn't the plan. I messed up bad. I'd trusted stupid Perdy, and she betrayed me." His body shuddered for a second.

"Your daddy."

I couldn't take the reference to daddy or father any longer. "He didn't raise me, so why don't we call him Mr. Briggs?"

His coal eyes narrowed, "*Mr. Briggs* couldn't know, so I said I disposed of your body and showed proof with your hospital hat. They accepted my proof, and no more was said. Then I had to find Perdy and you. Your mom, as you call her, was no angel - she was a junkie, loved to shoot it up into her arm." He spat the words at me like I didn't understand Perdy was a user and probably spent her half of the money on drugs. I kept my calm even though I wanted to strangle him behind the thick glass that separated us.

"I searched and couldn't find her until she contacted me, asking for money. She used pictures of you and threatened to tell your *daddy* if I didn't pay her. To get the amount of money she wanted I stole. I done many things but not theft. I got the money, but she didn't have you with her so I tailed her, hoping to get to you, but I lost her. Every three years she contacted me for money. I wanted to kill her but had to find and kill you first. Sneaky bitch, I always lost her. Finally, I decided that I'd had it!"

Anger oozed from the deep pitted pores that covered his face. "I killed her then searched for you. I strangled her and dumped her in the Sacramento River. It was easy, too easy. I searched for you and found you, almost by luck, with some boy. The two of you walking like you hadn't a care in the world - lovers." He chuckled. "I aimed my car for you but that stupid boy pushed you out of the way. Idiot! Your father knew everything including you bein' alive. Perdy sent pictures of you to him already. She set me up. Your *daddy* made sure I paid for my mistake." Hatred inside him boiled over and erupted in a verbal assault.

Even in his anger he was forthcoming, but not smart. I considered what Mr. Dancy Eyes, Mitchell Strat, said and thought it was an opportune time to give him a reason to be self-loathing. He hadn't mentioned Mr. Strat, and I became curious how he'd 'convinced him'. I continued my poker face, reminding myself to breathe normal. "I have one more question. For such a tough guy you gave yourself up easily and settled for a stay in this wonderful gray establishment." I leaned in and looked directly into his lump-of-coal-eyes. "Why? You could be free right now."

He narrowed his eyes, took in a deep breath then released it. His nose twitched while his glare dug deep into my bones sending a chill rippling down my spine. I held my ground. "It's not so bad. I have three square meals and access to the gym. It's not five stars but your tax money is payin' for it." I decided whatever Mr. Strat did, maybe it was better he didn't tell me and wanted nothing more than for Slug to get shanked in prison.

"I won't release the information as promised." Ready to leave, I hung up the phone and left. As soon as I got into my waiting taxi, I contacted La Tige and told him to release the information. I felt no remorse for setting up Slug. He deserved to spend the rest of his days behind bars.

Home Sweet Shack

After my visit with Slug I flew to Georgia and visited my mom's, Perdy's, grave. I brought a huge wreath of flowers and set them by her headstone. She raised and protected me to the best of her meager abilities. She died an ugly death by Slug's hand for me. In my opinion she deserved respect and my love.

Next, I boarded a plane and flew to where I remembered life beginning, to the shack. The town sprouted but not much. A couple new subdivisions developed, but Main Street looked almost the same except for a few stores changing names. The sight of Brennan brought back both pleasant and unpleasant memories. The night I decided to hop the train and set out on my own flashed in images through my mind. I saw a scared young girl who understood nothing outside of life in Brennan. She took a chance and against every odd survived and thrived.

My birth was an ordeal for many people and secrets popped out of the woodwork so the thought dawned on me to check the ownership of the shack. The idea so obvious I never considered it. I went to the courthouse and discovered the shack belonged to my sperm donor's wife's family. I wouldn't have guessed that, but it made sense. Claudel said, 'His wife knew about you, she knew about all his affairs but she had dignity and respect'. If aware of his affairs; why not any children produced from them? Obviously, she wanted me hidden. I imagine she wanted to protect her standing in the community. Maybe she even wanted to protect me or at least not have a dead child plaguing her conscious. For whatever reason, it boiled down to her self-preservation.

Slug blamed everything on Perdy who set him up but so did Mrs. Briggs. She sent Perdy and me here to live and may have partially financed our life. But she didn't pay the bills because the electricity got cut off leaving me with no power. The speculation grew tiresome. It didn't matter anymore.

From the outside, the shack had weeds as big as trees and plants overgrown to the point I sliced through them to get to the front door. Remnants of police crime scene tape stuck to the door and blew with the gentle breeze. The doorknob dangled, so I pushed the door open. It creaked and groaned as if saying *enter if you dare*. My heartbeat quickened and visions of Perdy's wild eyes, gaunt frame, and lifeless dull strawberry blond ponytail rushed through my brain.

The inside looked the same as I remembered reminding me of my life with Perdy. Cold baths, cheap boxed and canned foods, and my Perdy locked in her room. My body shuddered in an involuntary reaction. The couch I used as a bed still present with layers of dust settled upon it. One slow step at a time I edged towards Perdy's room. I sucked in a deep breath and pushed open her door. My last memories of this room were rummaging through her personal items, and finding empty bags of drugs, needles, and letters. The drawer full of needles and empty bags was barren. The police must have confiscated everything or teens using the shack as a hide-away-hang-out.

Tears busted forth like a waterfall from my eyes. I cried for Perdy, for myself, and for my love, Einstein. My return to the shack created an emotional upwelling inside me. One I hadn't expected. My body crumpled on the green sofa, dust particles covered the air surrounding me causing me to sneeze and cough. After several minutes or more, I pulled my laptop out of its bag, opened it, pressed the power button and typed. The words flowed with ease and refused to stop.

When my computer battery wore down, I walked into town and charged it at the local coffee shop while I continued to write. Before returning to the shack I stopped at the hardware store and purchased a new lock for the front door and cleaning supplies.

The shack used well water. When I turned the faucet orangish water sputtered from it. I left it running until it ran clear taking that time to replace the door lock. After scrubbing and beating the curtains, couch, and Perdy's bed the cabin looked perky and almost livable. My body spent for the day I laid on the couch and fell into a dead sleep.

Sunshine poured in from the front window awakening me out of my sleep. Refreshed I brought out my laptop and continued writing my memoirs. When the battery went low, I trekked into town again, charged it and grabbed food. It took days and boxes of facial tissue as I went back and forth from the coffee house to the shack. I wanted the world to know, and the truth exposed so I wrote my entire story from twelve years old to present.

I dug deep inside my backpack and relived every moment of my life on the run. While riffling through it I found the camera Einstein and I won many, many moons ago at the video game haven.

The batteries inside the camera were dead, so I plugged it into my computer, and hunted through the pictures of Einstein and I, reminiscing with tear clouded eyes for happy memories and loss. To my shock and horror, the shooting photos I forgot existed displayed vividly on the screen before me - guns, brains, and blood. I scanned them one by one reliving each frightening moment from that dreadful night. Ethically I understood I needed to do something. The pictures many years old couldn't be ignored any longer. The men might have families, friends who care and want answers. I saved the pics in a file on my computer. When ready I'd show them to La Tige.

Coffee filled my gut and fueled my brain during those days. It was the release my mind and heart needed to move forward in my life. When I finished, I mailed my manuscript to Einstein's family, remembering his mother gave me a business card and asked them to read and publish it. The proceeds donated to the MacCannaly Organization - a nonprofit organization whose sole purpose was helping children and young adults on the streets. I didn't want others to endure and suffer as I had.

I packed my belongings and got ready to leave taking one last look at the shack. As I touched the door lock voices on the other side of the door caught my attention. I'd been alone in the shack, coming and going for days, maybe weeks, and people now stood outside the door? I placed my ear against the cold wood door and listened.

"Thought you said it wasn't locked?" Said a girl's voice.

"It's not dumbass."

I moved the corner of the curtain aside and peered outside similar to how Perdy did it. A teen with curly brown hair and a slender build, his pants sagging and appearing unwashed, twisted his body toward the road. Then he said, "This path is new too."

The boy turned back towards the front, and I ducked. Then one of them attempted to open the window with no luck. I unlocked the door and slid it open.

"Can I help you?"

Both teens' eyes grew wide as dinner plates. The girl, chunky and freckled faced responded, "We uh... we didn't know." Then they looked to each other and ran away quick as a rushing river.

Jeez, now I had to find them. Their shabby appearance suggested both were runaways.

Catch Me if You Can

I searched the surrounding woods looking in all the nooks and crannies I would have hid inside of. My advantage, I played in the woods as a child and knew the best hiding places. I found them in a hollowed-out tree trunk, one of my favorite childhood spots. I walked up to the tree keeping my voice calm. "Come on out. I'm not going to turn you in."

One at a time they crawled out of the tree trunk. Both stood before me staring at the ground. "We're sorry. We didn't know you lived there." Said the girl.

"I don't anymore. What are your names?" Their eyes met then both sets locked onto my eyes.

"I'm Rosey and he's Thorn." Obviously made up names, same M.O. as Einstein and I.

"Rosey and Thorn, nice to meet you. Are you hungry?"

Thorn grabbed Rosey's hand. "Yes, thank you. What's your name?" I envisioned the many times Einstein held my hand in a similar way.

"Shanna, I don't drive but town is a short walk."

"Why don't you own a car?"

Rosey poked Thorn in the side and whispered, "She invites us to eat and you complain she doesn't have a car?"

I chuckled. "I don't like to drive."

We strolled into town and chatted most the way. Once we sat down for dinner they ate like little pigs, another sign confirming they ran away. When they filled their bellies, I asked them questions.

"I won't waste my time or yours. Rosey and Thorn are not your real names. I want to help you, but you have to trust me."

"We can leave, thanks for dinner," said Thorn.

I put my palm out instructing them to stop then waved my hand towards the seat for them to sit. They were compliant and planted their butts back into the booth.

"Spill."

Rosey opened her mouth first. "My mother is ill. She can't work and my father is dead."

I raised my eyebrow then turned to Thorn. "And you?"

He sat silent for a moment his head angled towards the table. He rose his head without looking at me. "OK, Rosey is a better liar than me. Her mother isn't ill, and her father isn't dead. We go into your cabin sometimes and smoke pot."

I nodded. "The made-up names?"

"We didn't want to get caught. It's still illegal for us."

"Unless you have a medicinal card which two minors wouldn't have. Where do you get the pot?"

Thorn shrugged. "My dad's stash."

"Do you live close?"

"I do, Thorn is my cousin. He's staying with me this weekend." Rosey slid out of the booth.

"I'll walk you both home."

Relief washed over my body until I saw Rosey's house. The siding missing in spots, junk cars littered the driveway, and the front window had a long crack in it. Poor didn't mean her parents weren't loving people. I sucked in my judgements until I met her parent's.

"Thanks, you don't need to follow us inside."

"I'd like to say hi to your parents."

An outside light lit up as we walked towards the house. And the front door opened. A bulky man stood in the doorway, blocking the inside light. "That you Jen?"

"Yes dad."

"Who's that with you?"

"Shanna, we met her in town today."

Her father carried his large bulk towards me. "Shanna, nice to meet you and thank you for seeing they got home safe. Would you like to step inside for a minute?" I accepted his offer as I worried for the teens. After thirty minutes of discussion he passed my test, and I left. The shack stood on the other side of the patch of woods from their house.

Crickets chirped their nighttime song, and the gibbous moon lighted my way. I stayed one last night. The next morning, I bought $346 worth of groceries and had them delivered to Rosey's (Jen's) house.

Freedom

I obtained a copy of my birth certificate; my birth name Camille Shariff. I wasn't fond of Camille but it was better than Babet Higgins, Perdy's name for me. Most times she called me Baby Girl or Baby. I never considered I always lived under a false name or where that name originated. No doubt Mrs. Briggs had a little something to do with our false identities. Thank the heavens my bio-mom didn't include my sperm donor's name or any part of his name in mine. Maybe my bio-mom had some good in her and wanted nothing from him. It didn't matter - a simple paternity test would have proven I was his child.

None of that mattered now. I legally changed my name to Cleo Burke with my true birthday and age - August 2, 20 years of age. I grew up believing my birthday to be May 2. I was a Leo not a Taurus! And I was a week shy of 21.

I hired a real estate agent and made a substantial offer on the property containing the shack.

It took a couple weeks for Mrs. Childrone to get back to me. Her email read:

Shanna,

Thank you so much for sharing your story and life with our son. I had no idea he meant so much to you. My heart is overjoyed. For many years we suffered in anguish with no idea what happened or why. Now we have closure. We share a love for Burke, Einstein, as you called him. I would like you to come to New York and stay with us.

We don't want to donate. We want to set up a nonprofit organization to help homeless children and would be honored if you would help us put it together.

Mrs. Childrone.

My eyes' flood gates opened again and a torrential downpour of tears flowed down my cheeks. After I pulled myself together, I hopped on the next flight to New York, back to the belly of the beast, only this time to set up an everlasting memory of Einstein.

Mrs. Childrone waited at the gate for my arrival. I wasn't sure how she pulled that off, but I welcomed her huge hug and the tears flowed freely. My body excreted so much fluid in the form of tears it surprised me that I hadn't shriveled into a human prune.

She took my face in her hands. "Shanna, you are such a beauty both inside and out. I can see why Burke loved you." She wrapped her arms around me again.

A limo waited for us outside the airport and we rode to their house in upstate New York, not their apartment in the city but their mansion. For a child raised in extreme poverty, I spent almost as much time schmoozing with the wealthy. The driveway to their house its own road, lined with well-manicured shrubs. The front door twelve feet high opened into a large foyer with a crystal chandelier bigger than me.

"Shanna, you can leave your bags by the door, Clarence will get them." A tall, thin, bald man smiled at me while collecting my bags then disappeared.

"Cleo, please." I reminded her.

"Yes, I'm sorry. Cleo. Burke's name for you."

"Now it's my legal name."

I followed her through the house as she showed me the kitchen, reading room, and other various nooks and crannies. Then she pulled a brass candle holder attached to the wall, and it opened. The wall slid backwards opening into a hallway. "This was Burke's favorite place. The hallway comes out at various spots throughout the house. He liked to run through it to get from one room to another. We put it in as a safety feature, but once he discovered it, to him it was a gateway to his imaginative paradise. Follow me."

She took me on a tour. G.I. Joes and Hot wheels lay scattered on the floor. I leaned down and touched a small toy truck. Its paint chipped and three wheels instead of four. "You can pick it up."

"These were his?"

Her eyes took on a distant glow as she remembered. "Oh yes, we left these hallways the way he left them. As he got older, he spent more time reading in here, but the toys were always a reminder of his innocence. Would you like to keep that truck?"

"May I?"

She nodded her head.

She pointed to various outlets and doorways that led to this and that room in the house. It was like an entire house hidden inside another house. I'd never seen anything like it. She pushed a door open, and we entered a room with shelves filled with crime books. I took one off the shelf and flipped it to the back cover, true crime. A full-size bed with a camel colored comforter and matching pillows sat in one corner and on a desk in a nook beside a window sat a dated laptop. A couple dressers lined the walls. Still holding the book, I asked the obvious, "This was his room?"

Her eyes curled in at the corners, a perfect match to her smile. "Yes."

A decade ago, I never would have imagined standing in a house this big, much less that my boyfriend lived here and ran away! I knew he had reasons, but after meeting his parents I couldn't understand why. The Childrones' were so normal, unlike my twisted wealthy family that, fortunately for me, didn't raise me. If I'd grown up with the insanity of my family I'd probably be as crazy as they are.

We left his room and Mrs. Childrone showed me to my room. "I have taken enough of your time today. I'm sure you need rest after the long flight."

"Thank you. A shower maybe." I lay back on the bed in awe. What forced him to leave? Am I missing something?

For the next few days we met with various lawyers and accountants setting up the Einstein Fund. All proceeds from my book would go to the fund along with a few million from Will's wire transfer. My selfish sperm donor's money would help children. And we set up strict stipulations stating how the money could be spent.

The marketing specialists wanted me to go on tour completing book signings across the U.S. I postponed that for the future. There were people I needed to see and speak with before I showed up at engagements and book signing events in cities across the country.

The past couple weeks a penetrating whirlwind that drained me in an emotional and physical sense but yet I couldn't sleep. My mind focused on Einstein's wonderful family. It wasn't them. He didn't leave because of them, I'm sure of that.

I found myself in his room. My body fell back on his camel covered bed, rolling his comforter around me as if it were his arms

and inhaled in the sweetness of his bed
seeking any lingering Einstein scent.
Instead, I smelled fabric softener. I bounced
upwards from his bed like an alley cat being
chased by a bulldog and ransacked his
room, searching for clues, anything to tell
me why he left.

I went through his drawers, tore his
books off his shelves one by one and found
nothing. Then I remembered the hallways!
Through his closet, I entered the passage
and must have walked through each
passage several times before a picture
caught my attention. It was Einstein and a
friend on what looked like a camping trip.
They looked about ten or eleven. I pulled
the picture off the wall and studied it. The
light caught a small bump behind the
picture, something was there. I took the
back off and a newspaper article dropped to
the ground.

On it a picture of the boy who was in
the picture with Einstein. He disappeared,
his dead body turning up on a hiking trail in
Oregon. Stuck to the inside back of the
picture frame was a map containing a list of
names and addresses I remembered from
my time running around the country with
Einstein. Each person wealthy and of high

importance, including the judge whose letter opener I stole by accident and returned by way of drunk bum.

I kept the map, the article and put the picture back, then checked every picture lining the passageways - more newspaper articles. I laid them out and read. The court tried the person arrested as the boy's killer, but with lack of evidence, they found him innocent. The judge on the case was letter-opener-judge. I read each article. They read almost the same - missing children, a few found dead. The list went on and the story swirled into clarity. Einstein's mother told me he wanted to be an FBI agent, and his friend mysteriously kidnapped and murdered. Many of the homes and cities we visited contained the missing children. He searched for clues to his friend's abduction and the other children.

Einstein's dated laptop called out to me. I plugged the cord into the wall and pressed the power button, it sputtered to life. I typed in *Einstein* as his password and it zoomed to the next screen. On a hunch I searched through every file, nothing, until I discovered an encrypted file. I felt the sides and back of the computer and bingo it had a USB drive, so I ran-tiptoed back to my room grabbed my flash drive then uploaded his documents to it.

My mind buzzed with activity; my body drained. I didn't yet understand the connection between the children if one existed, but I'd figure it out for Einstein.

I packed the articles into my backpack, which contained my memorabilia from my life on the run. Into my suitcase I placed seven copies of my book, which I purchased, and slipped my thumb drive into its slot in my computer bag and went to bed. My mind at peace.

Closure

I mailed a copy of my book to my sperm donor and another to my bio-mom. I wanted them aware of the pain, agony, and terror I endured as well as my success. A guilt filled trip for them down memory lane. The other five I was delivering in person. I called Glynn and met him at the park. He already knew most everything, I figured he might as well read the rest.

I boarded a plane and made a flash trip to San Francisco to see Kacy and La Tige and give them their copies. They greeted me with hugs and love.

"Oh my God!" Shouted Kacy, her voice filled with glee. She wrapped her arms around me giving me a huge hug.

I hugged her back as if we hadn't seen each other in years instead of months. I wasn't sure where to start but thought the beginning would be a great place.

"There is so much to tell you." I took her hands, flashing a can-you-take-over-the-bar look at Alex. He nodded his head, confirming he understood and placed the box of Miller in his arms on the floor then whipped up a drink for a customer. I guided her out the door and we walked up and down the hills as I began my life story. "Kacy, you are my best friend. I've kept a lot of secrets from you and everyone else…"

She stopped, her deep velvets peering into my soul. "I know Shanna-honey you have secrets; I just don't know what they are. You finally going to tell me?"

Nervous energy coursed through my body. I sucked in a deep bay filled breath then released. "First, I'm not really Shanna. I was kinda, but my name is Cleo. My birth certificate said Camille but I like Cleo. I'm rambling, telling the truth and friends, it's new to me…" That's how my come-to-truth moment started with my best friend. "Kacy, you're like a sister to me. I'm so sorry I never told you any of this foolishness before now."

"Sh… Cleo, that is weird to say. Honey I get it. I know you. You're OCD."

I jabbed her in the side then wrapped my arms around her neck and whispered in her ear, "Am not."

She giggled. "Maybe one day you'll see I'm right about Fetch too."

"Have you seen him or heard from him?"

She nodded her head no. "Your eyes lit up when I mentioned his name. He's gone. His apartment is empty. He vanished without a good-bye."

"So, he can stalk me in New York."

Each step we took brought us closer to Happy Trails until we stood outside the bar. Without words we hugged then walked inside. I grabbed the bag I left behind the bar and handed Kacy a copy of my book. "My whole life story is in the pages of this book. Love you."

She took the book and held it to her chest. "You're an author! I'm finding out secrets and hidden talents.

We snuck upstairs to the apartment and talked, watched movies, did each other's nails, and she dyed my hair back to dark brown. No longer did I need to hide.

The following morning, I went by La Tige's office to surprise him. His blue eyes lit up like I've never seen as I entered his office. "Nu! Back from New York. Plenty of work here to keep you busy."

I was speechless and ran to him wrapping my small arms around his bulk as he folded me into him. Tears flowed freely -

from me of course, not him. I sucked up my tears and in a broken, quivering voice said, "You and me, we may not be related by blood but you're the only father I've ever had. I love you!"

His eyes watered over for a second and a single tear escaped and ran down his cheek. "You're slobbering on my best suit."

I punched him in the hard block gut. La Tige folded me into him again. "Love you, Nu."

He said it. He admitted it! I had a father, not biological, but better, a man who loved me. I pulled my head out of his chest and looked him in the face. The deep blue of his eyes sucked me into the vast ocean of his warm soul and I felt a rush of discovery tingle my spinal cord. "How much have you known?" I asked, handing him a copy of my book.

He grabbed the book and nodded his head. "Not everything. But a lot."

"And you didn't tell me?"

"Would you have accepted it?"

He made a point and knew me better than I knew myself. "No."

"You left telltale clues on my computer, delete searches in the future."

We spent a few hours catching up, and I helped him organize his mess of an office.

Afternoon turned to evening as the sun's falling rays left trails across the sky. "Found a great new place, let's get a burrito." He threw his keys at me. "You're driving."

I threw them back and shook my head. "No way. That's your beast-vehicle."

We unrolled the windows allowing the San Francisco breeze to cool us. I remembered the pictures I found of the shooting Einstein and I witnessed. No time like the present to ask. "I have pictures... uh... I witnessed a murder and captured it with my camera. If I send you the... "

"Send em'."

"Thank you!"

"The investigative gene is part of your soul."

"My natural curiosity."

We ate burritos and ordered an extra then headed to Happy Trails where we found Kacy pouring over my book. A box of facial tissue beside her and a trash can within tossing distance. Kacy jumped up from her seat and ran towards me with extended arms then wrapped them around me.

The three of us enjoyed several beers and Kacy hugged me every chance she got.

The following morning, La Tige dropped me off at the airport. I needed to see James. He always helped me - discreetly. He was there when my Einstein died and gave me the life blood of a new ID to keep going. I had more than a book to give him, but a life blood to him and LulaBell. My plane landed, and I jumped on the first bus to the sleepy southern town.

I knocked on his door and James greeted me with a warm hug and smile. "No more orange. The brown suits you better. Certainly didn't expect you but you're always welcome."

About that time LulaBell came bounding forward. "Cleo!" She bombarded me with a hug.

They welcomed me inside and we sat on the little sofa beside the window. "I have no need to hide anymore..." That started our conversation. As the afternoon sun set, it left streaks of brilliant reds and golds in the sky, LulaBell went to the store for dinner supplies. She wanted to cook for me. That's when James and I got a moment alone. I handed him a large new backpack stuffed to the hilt with hundreds and slid inside the front pocket, a copy of my book.

His eyes grew as large, "Wow! What - did you do, rob a bank?!"

I gave him a cheeky smile in return, followed by a giggle. "No, I'm rich. My bio-family is loaded and my ex-boss/brother passed a small fortune my way."

His dinner plate sized eyes shrunk to normal and a solemn expression took over his face. "It's now or never... time for my confession. Twenty years ago my sister gave birth to LulaBell. She was the happiest I've ever seen her. I was on my way over for an after-work visit. She could cook up a storm." He brushed his hand over his mouth and twisted his lips. "As soon as I parked my car a gunshot rang through the air. I rushed up the driveway and busted through the front door of her house. She lay on the kitchen floor, blood streaming from her head." He took a deep breath, then continued, "My brother-in-law stood with a gun in his hand. Anger boiled inside me. He took a shot at me but his hand was so unsteady that I dodged it. I did something I'm not proud of."

He paused for a second and my heart stopped as I knew what he was about to say.

"With my bare hands, I choked him until the life drained out of his eyes. When my anger subsided, I took LulaBell, and we spent her first several years on the run. I changed our identities many times until we found this town. Life seems to stand still here, and we started fresh. She was a few months old when it happened and doesn't know I'm not her father."

My heart choked at his story. "You are her father. You raised her. If you hadn't killed her bio-dad, who knows what type of life she would have grown up living? You love each other and she is an amazing young woman. I searched for my bio-family for years only to realize they consist of people with no genetic or blood connection to me, except William. You did what you did for your niece."

He smiled as water filled his eyes and he nodded his head. He'd been there when Einstein died, now it was my turn. I stood up and wrapped my arms around him. He was like an uncle to me.

"Thank you." He whispered.

LulaBell came home, cooked us a wonderful meatloaf, and we talked the night away. I ended up crumpling on their sofa and spending the night.

The next day I embarked on a journey that took me across the Atlantic by way of a cruise to France. Being alone gave me time to think about my life and events put into action and their consequences. Mrs. Briggs' self-preservation, but wasn't that what drove everyone? They fought to take care of themselves, leaving a defenseless child to care for herself - selfishness. My poor, naive mom, Perdy probably considered Slug the love of her life; her knight in shining armor who saved her from an abusive father. He turned out to be pure evil, and she fought for survival until he killed her. I can't forget she fought for me.

My birth mother who knowingly had an affair with a married man and then became pregnant with a child she could never raise - a kept woman. I followed in her footsteps and became Didier's kept woman. The difference, Didier was a single man. He took care of me, yes, and loved me, but married - no. His mistake was falling for a young woman with a screwy past life. My sperm donor paid my bio-mom and gave her a brownstone where she still lives. She made a choice to accept his gifts for silence and didn't fight for the baby she birthed.

My sperm donor wanted me dead to preserve his financial security. His birthright in the family business meant more to him than anything. Women deceived Slug, over and over; first by my mother, Perdy and Mrs. Briggs and then by me. He thought he needed to keep me a secret and my bio-father might not have known, but his wife did. My life started with an impossible situation and I didn't know all the players or the cards, but I survived. I ran, changed identities, and varied my looks. Einstein and I stole jewelry and items from people's homes and sold them for money. I have done whatever necessary to survive just like everyone else.

It's difficult to let go, no matter how much or how little we have. The only truths in my life were the men who loved me. One, who searching for his own hidden answers, died for me and the other I ran away from, seeking answers, self-preservation. Fetch was Fetch. If we had something real will always be a mystery because I never gave it a chance.

My past behind me now, I took the stolen jewelry out of my worn backpack and placed it in a purple Crown bag I talked one of the cruise ship bartenders into giving me. For years I held onto the stolen goods. A necessary security for a lost girl who didn't want to live on the streets, eating leftovers, trash, and sleeping in tiny holes. As I child, I understood no different. Now I did. I dropped the jewelry over the side of the ship into the ocean and watched it sink. It made a small splash and ripples of water emanated from the core. Then it vanished. I'm sure the jewelry meant something to someone somewhere but mine and Einstein's fingerprints were all over it - our ticket off the streets. If I remembered who it belonged to, I'd have given it back, but I didn't remember.

I spent almost a decade trying to unravel the secrets of my past, my identity. But it's been with me all along, whether Einstein's Cleo, Justine or Shanna. I always thought I had to put on an act to bring my identity to life but I was always me, simply me.

I pondered on how my life may have turned out different if Perdy hadn't taken me; if I grew up with my bio-mom. Would I have ever met Einstein or traveled to Paris alone at 16? Probably not. Would my life have been better? Most definitely not! My life, and who I am, are defined by events put into action before my birth and I'm not sorry for the life I've lived. I am not sorry for my life with Perdy, my crime spree across America, or my life with Didier.

By sheer stubbornness and determination, I discovered the dark secrets of my past and met people whom I love and I'm stronger because of my love and losses. If one event in my life happened different my life would be on a changed path. I developed from my experiences and they shaped my soul. I wasn't just Cleo Burke, I was me. Cleo, no longer in hiding and standing up for myself on my own two feet.

When the ship docked in France I went straight to Didier's hotel. I stood outside for about thirty minutes, trying to gain the courage to enter. As I stepped one foot inside shockwaves of insecurity shot through my veins, the grandness of the hotel came rushing back at me. The first day I met Didier teetered in my conscious mind becoming a full-blown memory. I waltzed in off the streets expecting to get a room. As a street urchin I didn't realize I needed to 'make a reservation'. The butterflies went crazy in the pit of my stomach, mixed with flashbacks of the day we met.

The butterflies in my belly replaced with sorrow. Tears formed beneath my eyes. I fought them back as I wandered into the enormous lobby.

Everyone bustled around and customers talked, strolling into and out of the shops, restaurant and bar. I didn't see Didier anywhere. I knew there was a chance he wouldn't be present. He owned other hotels often taking him away on business. I went to the bar and ordered a glass of French wine. I drank glass after glass until my head became light. From across the hotel lobby someone caught my eye, Didier. He made small talk with his customers in the restaurant. I watched until he caught my glance. Our eyes met, and the seconds froze. Every part of my being wanted to jump into his awaiting well defined arms. His gaze changed from jovial to gloomy and he disappeared.

Common sense gained control. What the heck was I doing? It was a mistake for me to be here! My presence would devastate his life again or at least send it spiraling through memory lane. After leaving him at the altar my actions were unforgivable! I just couldn't hurt him again. Maybe he disappeared to avoid me. I used him and threw him away, a genetic talent. I left before offering him the chance to verify if it was me. Before walking out the door, I stopped at the front counter and left him a package. A copy of my book and note that read...

I want you to understand why,
Love Justine.

My crazy moment ended, never to return. I climbed into a cab and headed to the airport. I didn't know what I thought would happen when Didier saw me, but for the best it didn't happen. Our relationship was a lifetime ago, in another world. I cried for the umpteenth time in a few short weeks; my tears busted loose like a dam bursting with water. John Legend and "All of Me" poured from my backpack. Perfect timing Fetch!

I ignored the ring, wallowing in my memories of another man and cried the entire drive to the airport. The taxi driver looked at me through his rear-view mirror a couple times but never said a word. I didn't want to be bothered instead I wanted to curl up and become as small as possible. For years I fought back the tears, now they flowed, and I lacked the ability to make them stop. When the waterfall stemming from my eyes subsided, I boarded the next flight desperate to leave Paris. As the plane taxied the runway and lifted its nose into the air fun-filled memories entered my mind. My next stop...

Caribbean Heat
Baby Girl Book V
Paradise

Our backs laying on the sandy shore behind my St. Thomas house. The edge of the tide drifted over our feet and receded.

"Do you ever think you'll give her a chance?" asked Will, my half-brother. Born from the same father who, in my opinion, is a wicked, vile man. My dislike for him conflicted to the millionth degree with my sense that, in his own demented way, he loved me.

"I don't know. How could she let me go? She never searched, just took your - our - father's word for it. Since when does he tell the truth?" I glimpsed my bio-mom once, that's it, but couldn't bring myself to meet her. In my heart I knew I was tougher on her than my sperm donor father.

Will chuckled, his blond hair blowing in the breeze as he turned and lifted himself onto his elbows and turned towards me. "You're right. He doesn't tell the truth often. He is a tough, conniving man who's become more reserved since," he cleared his throat, "your last meeting." The last time I saw my sperm donor I intentionally poured red wine down his white, expensive dress shirt. It felt incredible!

I twisted onto my stomach and lifted myself onto my elbows and peered at Will through the long tufts of hair whipping across my face. "My entire life is like a daytime soap opera. Now it's my time… I've been many people: born as Camille, then Cleo, Justine and Shanna, and I won't mention mom-Perdy's name for me, now I'm legally Cleo Burke. I'm no longer that scared young girl with no roots, but a grown woman who wants nothing more than to put my past behind me and move forward with my life."

His eyes scanned the vast Caribbean. "I see. I've never seen such clear ocean water. This place makes me want to stay and say F-it. The business doesn't need me!" His voice mingled with the sound of the tide beating against the shore.

"Yup, why I chose it. It's breathtaking and the beaches are pure and crowded with palm trees. Dense, lush green plants cover the Earth. And the sunrise and sunsets are incredible." The sun lingered just above the ocean, sinking beneath the horizon. The colors of the sky reflected from the ocean giving our eyes a breathtaking visual display.

We lay silent as the sun set over the ocean and the tide rolled in and out over our bodies. I bought a small beach house in St. Thomas. I had a home, a real home. It was small and modest but it was mine. It had three bedrooms and two baths separated by a vast expanse enclosing my kitchen, dining room and living room. Each bedroom accommodated a walk-in closet and my bath included a large tub with jets much like the one I enjoyed while living with Didier. And hot water - tons of hot water. A small bar stocked with fine wines and various rums separated the kitchen from the living room.

My decorations were light, as I liked the open airiness of my home. I framed pictures of myself and Einstein into a collage. A large screen door in the living room opened into a small patio and the beach just beyond, where Will and I lay now in the sand. I spent my time staring at the ocean and island skipping. Thanks to my brother's generous $250,000,000 and shares in the family business. I considered it back child support from my sperm donor.

Will visited whenever he got the chance. We adored each other. He's the only member of my bio-family I desired to spend time with, and we shared it together acting like young children, catching up on the play time we missed. We golfed on the beach and when balls got pulled into the ocean the tide always brought them back. We learned to surf together, at first we did lots of falling off our boards together, but we've improved our skills.

Will stood and dusted the sand from his legs. "The sun is set - s'mores time." He strolled towards my patio, sand jumping from his feet with each step, and came back with wood.

While he tended to the fire I stood, not bothering to dust myself off, and padded inside to my pantry for Graham crackers, chocolate bars, marshmallows, and pokers.

My hands loaded with sweet treasures, I sat in the sand beside Will. "Whenever you tire of New York or divorce your bulldog wife," I looked at the scowl that washed across his face with the mention of his better half, "you always have a home here."

"Bulldog? Hmm... I think she's aged to look more like a Rottweiler." He guffawed, flashing brilliant, happy, green eyes my direction.

I met his laugh with a grin that took over the lower half of my face.

"So when is uh... Mr. La Tige coming in?" Will's visit was due to his eagerness to meet the fatherly figure in my life, La Tige. A man of few spoken words whose body language and heartfelt gestures say he loves me. I'm the daughter he never had. Will was staying long enough to meet him. He had to get back to New York and business before our evil demon-spawn sister, Patrice, found a loophole to take over the business and leave us out in the cold. Ha! I'd been there.

"Tomorrow. We're meeting him in San Juan and I've planned a small vacation excursion for him. He never relaxes like someone else I know." I shifted my eyes, giving him a sideways glance. "Someone with blond hair that has a blow over right now from the wind." He was always sensitive about his inherited male pattern baldness. The only trait he picked up from our father.

"You!" Is all he got out as I shoved my s'more into his gaping mouth. More of it landed on his lips and beneath his nose, giving him a s'mores mustache.

I fell backwards into the sand in laughter and found his s'more planted in my mouth. More s'mores made it into my mouth because it was open wide enough for a jet engine to fit! Pain from laughter shot though my abs as though I did a thousand crunches with weights tied to my chest. He leaned over and offered me a hand covered in s'more that he'd wiped from his face. "Eww... You gave me cooties!" I leaned over to wipe the mess on his chest but he was too quick and slid backwards out of my reach.

"Yeah, it's time!" I voiced with seriousness and rose to my feet, sauntering inside the house. After washing my hands, I made two mudslides loaded with spiced rum. Rum was the way of the islands and I grew to love it.

I took my spot beside him on the beach, the vast Caribbean spread out before us, the tide humming as it rolled in and out. I handed him his drink and rested my head on his shoulder. Where we sat in silence admiring the visual display before us.

Black Widow

La Tige stepped off the plane in San Juan, as always, looking out of place in paradise. In the past I've tricked him into small cruises within the islands and we've dined on native Caribbean foods. It's not often I see him but he is my surrogate father and I love him as much as Will. Last visit I teased him about his attire. The Caribbean was a place of comfort and warm weather. His usual disheveled suit made him stand out. He took my advice this time and wore a polo shirt, shorts and flip flops, but his uptight gruffness still showed.

People in Puerto Rico worked on their own time clock and were always friendly. They didn't seem to understand the hustle and bustle of the states. I admired that about island life because, even though on U.S. soil, one would never know. It was like a foreign country all its own. I planned on keeping him in PR (Puerto Rico) for a couple days before heading to St. Thomas. I always picked him up here, but we never stayed, always heading to VI (Virgin Islands) in a rush, but not this time. There was so much to do and I made a goal to show him the richness of the island and provide him an actual vacation. I booked reservations at one of the most renowned resorts in the San Juan area and booked a limo to transport us from the airport into another world, resort life in PR.

He held a single carry-on bag, he packed light as he never stayed long; he walked towards me and wrapped an arm around my back in a half hug. Affection was not a strong point for La Tige but underneath he was like a child's much-loved stuffed toy.

Will looked him over pensively and La Tige returned the visual cues. "Overprotective brother Will, meet surrogate overprotective father."

"La Tige." He extended his hand towards Will.

"Will. Pleasure to finally meet you Mr. La Tige." Will accepted La Tige's hand in a friendly shake.

"Now that's over with, how was the trip?" I asked.

"Long,"

"So, what is on our agenda?" La Tige asked with undertones of *I know you have something planned.*

I smiled. "You know me too well. We are catching a limo back to a resort and you are taking an actual vacation."

"Glad I cleared my calendar for a couple days. Every time I visit you it's never simple. You are not simple." He countered with inflections of intrigue.

William piped in, shaking his head in dismay, "Women are never simple."

La Tige chuckled and turned his large bulk towards Will. "Never."

"I am what I am and you," I shifted my eyes from Will to La Tige, "will always be you. I want you to share in this alluring world in which I live. Look around you, is there anything more breathtaking in all the world?"

"No, I don't think there is." They responded in unison then stared at each other...

The limo driver waited where Will and I left him, he opened the doors for us while he took La Tige's single bag of luggage and stowed it in the trunk.

For a world lacking mainland hustle and bustle, the roads stayed packed with cars, making any trip slow going. It gave Will and La Tige a chance to talk.

At dinner that night we ate a delicious authentic meal with tostones on the side - one of my favorites - and I ate them like one might eat potato chips. They are a simple recipe of mashed, fried plantains and are delightful. After dinner we relaxed on the beach with drinks. Fine French wine would always be my favorite but, like any place, PR had its version of fine alcohol- rum! The rum here isn't just rum, but a recipe they have made into an art. I grew to love a good Mojito; my choice of fine Caribbean drink. La Tige was much simpler and drank rum and cokes. Will settled on drinking the local beer, Medalla.

I was on cloud nine spending the evening with the two most important men in my life! A refreshing breeze blew from the ocean.

Will and La Tige got along like old friends sharing silly Cleo stories at my expense. After several drinks and light conversation, Will stood. "I have an early morning, good night, sis." I stood and gave him a hug and peck on the cheek. "Mr. La Tige, take care of her. She's a fragile one." I kicked his shin, causing him to scowl playfully.

"Night." La Tige, still sitting, extended his hand and pulled Will in for a quick half hug.

I returned to my seat and La Tige leaned towards me and with a gentle voice, not a usual attribute, he said, "Thank you for doing all this. I don't take vacations or slow long enough to enjoy life."

"You're welcome. You've done many things for me and I want to give you a little back. This place is like no other. It's easy to lose one's self and, in return, bring one closer to who they are."

"I don't say it, but you are special to me. Many years ago, I was a different man, young and hopeful. A different man indeed. I was married." He paused for a long moment. "She was exquisite, but as a cop I couldn't give her the life she desired. She came from a family of wealth and luxury; she became pregnant. One night while I was on duty, I got a call. The hospital admitted her. She had a miscarriage. I hadn't been there for her, instead I spent the night amid a huge domestic battle involving firearms and injured innocent people. By the time I got to the hospital she'd vanished." His blue eyes distant. In his mind he was in the hospital with her all those years ago.

"The baby was a girl. She would be about your age. I buried her in San Francisco in a tiny coffin. She is the reason I've never left. I like being close to her. In my heart you share a place with her."

His stone exterior needed chiseling to break. Everyone owns their secrets. La Tige hinted at his but refused details until now. I thought of Didier and how I left him at the altar, dissolving from his life forever. La Tige's passion and loss flowed through my heart. "I'm flattered. You're like the father I never had. You and Will are my family. Your wife... has she ever... " I fumbled for the right words, choosing La Tige bluntness. "What happened to her?"

"At first it was too painful. I grieved the daughter I would never know and my wife who abandoned us. Anger boiled inside me! Years went by and I made detective, a case took me close to her or part of her. When she vanished from the hospital her trail went cold. She ceased to exist." His blank eyes stared into the vast ocean.

"You've read my book. I did something similar. I left Paris the night before my wedding and came back to the States assuming the identity of Shanna Nu. That's when we met. I loved Didier but my past was too shady and I didn't know my own identity. How could I keep running from my past and live in a fantasy world with a husband who didn't know the *real* me? It didn't seem fair to him. I went back to Paris before settling in the Caribbean."

I paused for a second. My past was no secret to La Tige, but not my quick Paris trip I kept that secret. "I made a whirlwind trip to Paris and walked into the hotel. I wanted to say sorry for being a fool, enjoy the delight of his strong arms around me again, and hear him say everything was OK, he loved me regardless. But I realized that was a child's fantasy. I loved him but wasn't "in love" with him. I was a kid. He made my life with him a fairy tale. After years of searching I found my identity. I left a copy of my book on the concierge counter and jumped a plane to the American mainland and finally the Virgin Islands."

I took a moment to formulate my next words. "Maybe she left to deal with her grief or escape a past like me and realized she was wrong to drag you into the twisted drama?" The romantic Puerto Rican music mimicked our conversation.

"Yes, she had a past, no woman that beautiful and exotic marries a man like me unless they are running." He stated, then deviated into the here and now. "I have a job for you if you're interested?"

The pound of the tide steady in the background, but our trip down memory lane and precious father daughter moment expired. Taken aback, I'm not sure how his mind shifted gears in just a few seconds. I stumbled over my words, making the transition. "I… uh… OK, what is the job?"

"I wouldn't ask, but I got a couple cases back home I need to close. The one I need you on has led me here, right here to PR. You must have read my mind when you booked this thing. An older couple visited me last week. Their son died of a heart attack and his widow sold his estate, took the money and vanished into thin air!"

His eyes met mine to make sure I followed his words. "It turns out the husband was a health nut and took a physical a few weeks prior to his death which showed his heart in absolutely perfect health. So how does a healthy guy die of a heart attack? And why does his wife disappear? You can understand why I took this case. His parents gave me a photo. I traced her - booked on a cruise here under an assumed name. The ship will dock here in three days. The next two, we will do whatever you want." His voice excited over the new case.

"Do you have her photo with you?" The wind whipped my French braid over my shoulder.

"Yeah, back in the room. I'll show you later. You interested?" He pushed my braid back to its spot behind my head.

"Yeah I'm interested! So, my job is to find and observe her; take some inconspicuous tourist photos?"

He held my chin in his oversized hand, sincerity in his voice. "Yes, but be careful. If she murdered him, she could be dangerous and I don't want you caught in the middle."

I looked into his sapphire blue eyes. "I understand, I can take care of myself, and I promise to be careful, you have my word."

With a chuckle, he said, "Yes, you can - better than any woman I have ever known - but careful isn't in your repertoire."

I leaned over and put my small arm around his wide back and my head on his shoulder. He reciprocated and gave me a kiss on the top of my head. The world stopped, and we shared a father and daughter moment on the beach. The tide now dangerously close to our feet.

At that moment in time, I believed my life mysteries solved, but deceit runs rampant in my genetics. My heritage is the spawn of evil spun out of control.

Play Time

I woke up in the morning to the unforgettable full-bodied aroma of Puerto Rican coffee. I had booked us into a two-bedroom suite. As I drowsily sauntered out of my room, I could see he was already up, sitting on the balcony which sported gorgeous views of the Atlantic. I poured myself a cup of coffee and sat down in the chair beside him.

"Morning. This is ass kickin' coffee!" he exclaimed.

Still half asleep, I responded, "That it is". I wasn't a huge coffee drinker, but the coffee here was out of this world; it didn't even require sugar and cream to make it drinkable.

"I need to ditch my clothes and fill my suitcase full of it," he chuckled.

It was meant as a joke but I pictured him doing it and customs confiscating it.

He continued, "What's on the agenda for the day?"

"I booked us on a tour of the rain forest. It's unbelievable," I stated.

He looked at his clothes carefully and responded, "I didn't bring any hiking clothes".

Giggling, "They have tour buses, but you can hike if you want."

"What time is this tour?" he asked.

"Eleven o'clock." I retorted.

He bellowed, "We have time to eat then, I'm famished! Not much of "a morning person" are you?"

"Nope, never have been," I sluggishly responded, remembering the many times he would call me in the early hours when I worked for him.

He was up and ready, so I finished my cup of coffee and showered, making myself presentable. We had breakfast at the resort. I had eggs and toast and he had the works - steak, eggs, potatoes, and more coffee. I drank more coffee as well while he finished. I wasn't much of a breakfast person either. Usually I ate more of a brunch.

The trip to the rain forest took a bit of time since it was on the east side of the island, but was fully worth it. The drive alone offered a landscape of flat-topped homes and businesses open on all sides. The views from the top of the rain forest were impressive. Looking out from the top was a blanket of trees on all sides and we stood amidst the clouds. The animals blended so well into their surroundings that it took a keen eye to catch them. Amongst the waterfalls were pools of water surrounded by an elaborate framework of vegetation. The coquí sing the song of the rain forest. They are everywhere, but good luck trying to find one.

"Can't find sights like this in San Francisco!" he roared.

"Definitely not, I think it's one of the most amazing places on Earth." I agreed with a lively tone.

"Those frogs, what are they again?"

"The coqui."

He replied with a puzzled tone, "Yeah, they make quite a racket, but it's oddly relaxing."

"If you promise not to make fun of me," I gently jabbed him in the side, "I have a CD with rain forest sounds. When I'm having trouble sleeping, I listen to it and within a few minutes I'm asleep."

With a great, huge smile he said, "Do you dream of little frogs?"

"Occasionally," I answered in my most smart-ass voice.

After the rain forest we ate a lunch-dinner combo. I had always been astounded by the amount of food he could pack into his gut. We ate in San Juan and the food was genuinely authentic. Resort food wasn't always the same quality and very overpriced. After, we meandered around and went into some of the shops. He bought coffee, surprise, and several different brands. My mind went back to my earlier vision of customs confiscating it. Well if they did, I would have to mail him some. We caught a cab and headed back to the resort for drinks on the beach.

The following morning, I awoke once again to the luscious scent of coffee. I had planned a "man" day of deep-sea fishing. We caught the boat just in time, and headed out over the blue vibrant waters while the crew explained all the ins and outs. It was a relaxing day and I was the only female. Even had I been interested; I couldn't have competed with fish; although the captain had seemed to take an interest in me. He was local. I could tell by his accent, but he spoke English quite well. Most everybody involved in tourism did. He had thick, wavy brown hair that hung just below his shoulders.

As the day went on, his waves became tangles and he eventually put them into a ponytail with strands of curls that hung loose. His eyes were like dark chocolate fudge. He took his shirt off once we got out into the open ocean and his torso looked like a well carved statue; lined in muscles that extended to his shorts which hung just below his hips. He kept a close eye on me, ultimately making small talk.

His name was Raul and he was local, as I had suspected. Just a couple years ago he had purchased his boat and started chartering deep sea tours. He only worked with a couple of the resorts but hoped to buy more boats and work with more resorts eventually. I told him I was from St. Thomas and was here on vacation with a good friend. I didn't want to give him too many details. Before we departed, he offered me his card and mentioned that he did private charters and I could call anytime.

As we walked away from the boat I could see La Tige was all smiles. He looked at me and said, "I think someone took a shine to you."

"You think? He gave me his card and told me to call anytime," I said, flashing the card in front of his square face.

"I'd say the feeling was mutual, you were lit up like a Christmas tree," he laughed out.

"OK, he was a really," I drug out the word really, "good looking guy and he was polite and maybe I'll call him sometime." I hadn't been too interested in finding a man. My past luck was not the greatest and Fetch had been the last one I'd seen during our little romp in New York.

"I'm ready to eat again; what do ya say?" he belted.

I was glad he changed the subject. I loved him but I wasn't too sure about offering details of my nonexistent sex life. We were both exhausted and ordered in - the wonders of room service. The last couple days had almost reminded me of my time in Paris. I loved the magic of the Caribbean. The crystal waters and pounding tide always brought memories, which really didn't make sense since I had never spent any time on the beach until moving here, but there was something here, something bewitching. I guess La Tige had felt it too, as he shared with me how glad he was that I done this for him. He said, "Maybe one day I'll retire and move here. I haven't been this relaxed in decades!"

I unhinged my body from the comfort of the chaise and he snickered, "Hey Nu, no frogs tonight?" I was now legally Cleo, but he still called me Nu. Old habits die hard. I picked up the pillow positioned just below the rim of the chaise and threw it at him. As I tarried to the bedroom, I heard him laughing.

www.ingramcontent.com/pod-product-compliance
Lightning Source LLC
Chambersburg PA
CBHW050541190726
48284CB00003B/1163